Also by Philip Jamieson

Imaginary Friends: The Importance of Being Fictional

Sausages and Mash: Short Plays for Pairs and Groups

Fish and Chips: Monologues for Acting Examinations, Auditions and Drama Lessons

All Day Breakfast: Duologues for Acting Examinations, Auditions and Drama Lessons

Beans on Toast: Monologues for Acting Examinations, Auditions and Drama Lessons

Hotcakes: Short Plays for Drama Lessons, Examinations and Competitions

Bacon and Eggs: Short Plays for Pairs

Essential Drama Skills published 1998 by First and Best in Education Ltd

Back to Basics published 1998 by First and Best in Education Ltd

New Essential Drama Skills published 2016 by First and Best in Education Ltd

A GCSE Drama Course Book published 2000, 2012, by First and Best in Education Ltd.

DOROTHY BEAR EDUCATION

Ghostly intruder or trick of the light? See 'The Ghost of Cassiobury Park'.

PHILIP JAMIESON

FOLKLORE DETECTIVE

Solving the Supernatural

For Sarah and Martin

Acknowledgements

Cover image by Raland/Shutterstock.com

The author would like to thank Elizabeth Jamieson for her advice and creative input.

The author also wishes to thank Barry Crisp for his assistance and Duncan Robinson for The hanging nun photograph.

Contents

Photographs

The Five Folklore Detecting Rules

1. Just because the evidence hasn't been uncovered, doesn't mean it isn't there.

2. If there's been no earlier mention of it, I'll assume that's when the lie started.

3. If it turns out not to be a hoax, I'm going to work out where the misunderstanding came from.

4. I'm only going to investigate weird stuff in a place where they serve good beer and decent pub food.

5. I will ignore all the tourist-luring tosh and look at the evidence.

The Bloodied Font

When I started out as a folklore detective, I was fearless and unflappable. I would stop at nothing to get to the truth of all sorts of weirdy, oldie-time cobblers. I'm talking about those dodgy tales that've been passed off as traditional legends or lore. Others have surprisingly humorous or disturbing origins. My twin loves, of old legends and good beer drove me onwards to visit folky hot spots all over this land.

It's no coincidence, I think, that the locations which yield the best folklore stories seem to brew the finest beers. I'm not just talking about my stomping ground of England. It's everywhere you look. In The USA, Europe, Asia, and Australia, booze and talking bollocks seem to go hand in hand.

And I'm not just talking about any old casual twaddle, hastily baked porky-pies, or well-worn wind ups. These lies were created by folk who can hold their beer, who come from long lines of seasoned tricksters. The fibs I'm referring to are on an epic scale. There are back stories, eyewitnesses, multi-faceted plots, and genuinely chilling twists. These stories were the work of creative people, their imaginations loosened from the constraints of sobriety by good ale.

Contrary to what we've been told by Historians, life in ye olden days wasn't a constant, tooth and claw struggle to survive for 'ordinary' folk. There was leisure time too. The village pub was always a place for talk. In Winter, shorter days meant less time in the fields, and more time in the boozer, prattling on about any old twaddle. The places must have been jam packed. Fuelled by local strong ale and warmed by your neighbours' body heat, fairy tales and legends aplenty spewed forth. It's still going on.

I've seen it happen. Thirty years ago, at a pub in a little village called Urchfont. I had been driving back to Devizes with a girlfriend. We liked the look of the place, so we stopped. There were eight men in the bar, farm workers we guessed. They were sat together, huddled around two small circular tables. As expected, their animated conversations stopped abruptly, and, after the obligatory staring, their interest in us seemed to wane. We ordered our drinks and Jane and I commented on how lovely Urchfont was. The landlord seemed pleased with the compliment. I asked him if he knew how Urchfont got its unusual name. This brought a broad smile to his big, friendly face.

"Sandy can tell it better than me", he answered.

He beckoned over a big, ruddy-faced slab of a bloke, wearing a well-worn jacket and a flat cap. Sandy broke away from the local pack and joined us at the bar. He brought his mug of beer with him, so I reckoned we were set for a proper tale. The other seven watched us with renewed interest.

Sandy was about fifty, I'd say. He was tall, with big sticky out ears and smelled like a damp dog. He made himself comfy on a stool whilst the landlord refilled his pint mug. Jane and I remained standing, our faces rapt with interest. Sandy was completely silent though.

3

We waited, smiling weakly. It was the most awkward thirty seconds or so that I've ever experienced. I briefly exchanged looks with Jane. She seemed to be (almost imperceptibly) nodding towards the till. Oh! Bloody Hell! I suddenly clicked. Pay for his drink! That's what he was waiting for.

I placed a fiver on the bar top, pushed it across to the landlord, and Sandy began to speak.

The village, he told us, was originally called Tockington. In the 11th century, though, the lady of the local manor had, at long last, given her lord a male heir. He was so delighted (and not a little relieved) that he paid for a new pulpit and font for the church.

The font was particularly impressive, built from imported Italian marble, and with a beaten gold basin. Her ladyship had designed it herself, a place fitting for her baby's baptism.

Her husband's generosity didn't end there though. He also turned over several of his acres to the village people – that's the inhabitants, not the 1970s band – for common land. In return, the locals unanimously agreed to rename the village 'Church Font', in tribute to her ladyship's ornate marvel.

All the signs were rewritten. Tragedy, though, swift, and ruthless, caused that cursed name to be changed once more.

It wasn't until the baptism itself that His Lordship actually saw his son unswaddled for the first time. It was traditional, back then, for a baby to be wrapped in

4

swaddling clothes most of the time. He saw, to his utter horror, unlike himself, the boy had bright red hair. Coupled with the striking violet-grey eyes, both were features of his chief groom. His Lordship was bloody furious, to say the least.

His wife froze in horror as she realised that he'd grasped the truth. His Lordship grabbed the child and, with one swift brutal movement, dashed his brains out against the marble font. The congregation screamed. His wife fainted.

In the chaos that followed, having retrieved his sword from the entrance, His enraged Lordship rammed it through his spouse's neck. He then demanded that the church be emptied, and that his swordsmen find the groom.

The groom, obviously having sensed which way the wind was blowing, had already gone into hiding. His Lordship had the font destroyed and, later on, the village folk removed the CH from signs, renaming the place Urchfont. No associations with that cursed baptism were to remain in their community.

Nine hundred years later, all had vanished of that tragic story except the village's name. His Lordship had died from the plague on a crusade, his line having died out. The church itself had burned down hundreds of years ago. Sandy told his story well.

The other drinkers listened, it seemed, with hushed reverence, to a story they must have heard many times before. Or had they? What if it was as new to them as it was to us? What if Sandy just launched a legend, there and then?

Thoroughly entertained, we left the pub and headed for Devizes. Jane, the more observant of us two, asked if I'd happen to notice Sandy's bright red hair? A few lank strands were sticking out from under his flat hat, it seemed. I hadn't. Having given it more consideration though, I did remember his violet-grey eyes.

The more I thought about his account, the more I began to wonder if any of it was drawn from real events?

When I began investigating, way back in the 1970's, I decided that I was going to make it my business to sort the wheat from the chaff. Some folklore legends had grown from roots that ran deep into the past. They had some traces of the truth in them. The vast majority though were massive fibs. I was going to have to work out some ground rules for my folklore detecting.

I came up with five such rules. They're printed on page 1.

Cow Tipping, Crop Circles, and Hairy Hands: How to Create a Folklore Legend

The first thing I do when starting out on a case is to identify the earliest report (or eye-witness account) of a phenomenon. This is one good method of identifying the hoaxer who started the folklore fib.

Generally, if there's been no earlier mention of it, I'm going to assume there's a good chance, that's when it started.

I've put this hypothesis to the test. I figured that, if I could pull it off, others must have done it before me.

In 1973 I invented Cow Tipping. It had the kind of urban mythological appeal that really caught on. Forty-eight years later, Cow Tipping stories can still be found on both sides of The Atlantic. It's been reported on TV, social media platforms, YouTube, and in newspapers.

I got the idea for upside down cattle when driving with two college friends past a field of sheep. I spotted a large ewe, upturned and in a lot of distress. Two little wobbly-legged lambs stood at a distance, baaing frantically.

We parked up, hopped over the fence, and two of us manhandled the wide-eyed, shit-encrusted beast into a standing position. How she got upside down in the first place, I haven't got a clue.

The ewe was a lot heavier to move than we'd imagined, and one of my two pals commented that it was a good thing it wasn't a cow. That was where and when the

Monty-Pythonesque image of a field full of inverted cows popped into my head.

Knackered after our labours, we stopped at The Black Horse in Cherhill for beers. After a couple of 6Xs, the Cow Tipping scheme seemed to me like a sure-fire winner. There were so many questionable historic legends that have survived for ages in this country, why shouldn't my stupid idea take root? The durability of one of those stories gave me extra self-belief.

In the lounge of the Black Horse, there's a large painting of The 18th century 'Cherhill Gang'. Five completely naked blokes are depicted attacking the carriage of some rich folk that they'd stopped on its way through the village of Cherhill. They became quite successful at this. Suddenly faced with five butt-naked bandits, the traumatised passengers instantly handed over their valuables. It was only when the victims were called upon to identify their robbers that the genius of the highwaymen came to light. Not a single robbed passenger could remember anything about them other than their nudity.

This story is accepted as a piece of history by lots of people in Wiltshire. The gigantic painting of bare blokes is certainly a talking point for drinkers and diners in the pub, but it's really a load of cobblers. The fib had probably been inspired by some famous 18th century pirates who boarded their victims' ships in their birthday suits. I was sure that if I hung a gigantic picture of upside-down cows in its place, I could start a legend that'd run for hundreds of years.

I put my ideas to my two companions. Having known me for a while, they just smiled weakly, nodded agreement, and sipped their beers.

Edge of Insanity. Your (Un) Official College
Rag. No 101. 3rd December 1973

Here, in our sleepy little corner of rural
Lancashire, something weird is happening.
Since October, farmers all over this region have
awoken to find many of their cows upside down.
Yes. The phantom cow-tippers were at it again!
Again? It has happened before. Back in 1668,
according to one local paper, 'Many distressed
cattle were found upturned in their pastures.
Farmers are most perplexed and enraged by the
fearful state this mischief has left their cows
in.'
Another parish paper declared that troublesome
elves and pixies might be the cause. It seems
that, under cover of a moonless night, the
mischievous little buggers like to find cattle
that have fallen asleep standing up. Using their
magic, quick as you like, they flip the poor
unsuspecting cows over, and run away into the
night, giggling.
This week, local farmers are appealing to folk to
help them stop this outrage. They have offered a
bounty of £5 for every elf, pixie, or fairy corpse
delivered to The Farmers' Union office in
Skelmersdale.
£5 a head! That's a lot of beer money folks.
Hurry! Go grab a sack and a big-ass club.
    Phil Jamieson.

Page from my college magazine. 1973.

Ever the heel-dragger, I eventually got my act together, so, eight months later, Cow Tipping was born. Growing up, I'd read a lot of fairy tale folky stuff about elves and pixies playing tricks on people, stealing livestock, and generally dicking us about. I decided that'd be a good starting point for my own legend.

So, in that pre-internet, pre- smartphones decade, the speed at which the legend spread was surprisingly rapid. Within two years, I'd read retellings of my homemade mystery in magazines, books, and the press. There were naturally, variations, but it was essentially the same fib.

In my original story, it was a 17th century tale of mischievous elves that tipped over the unsuspecting cattle, leaving the poor cows helpless, at the mercy of the elements and predators. Surprisingly, as it was spread by others, the elves were replaced with plain old people, yobs who'd deliberately set out to cause bovine distress. Lots of similar cases have been reported since. Some actually supported with photographic evidence.

I must stress that I have never tipped a cow myself. I wouldn't dream of doing such an unkind thing. I once stroked a cow's nose, but that's about my limit.

There was, at that time, only one written account of Cow Tipping, invented by myself and published in my college's magazine. I claimed that the incidents had alarmed local farmers. Previously, I wrote, the same thing had occurred around the North of England in the year 1668. My sources, I wrote, were from two articles that had appeared in newspapers of the time. I quoted directly from one of them. It's worth bearing in mind that, during the

Christmas holidays, copies of my college's raggy little publication had found themselves in all parts of the UK, and quite a few abroad. It's likely that relatives or friends of my fellow students had casually perused the article. Keen to spread the idea, I had seldom missed an opportunity to relate the 'old' legend to just about anyone I met.

I needn't have bothered with that kind of legwork though. Cow Tipping as an actual 'thing' was already working its way, relentlessly, into the sensation-hungry imaginations of our 1980s, 90s, and 21st century minds.

It's staggering to think that this stupid idea that was the product of a couple of seconds reverie on my part had become something credible in the minds of the credulous. But, to be honest, it only takes one person's briefest speculation, their, 'Hey! What if I claimed that...' moment, to give birth to an enduring folklore legend that can dupe so many normally rational people into believing something that's so...well...unbelievable.

I've met the two local men, in Wiltshire who'd started the whole Crop Circle mystery. Both chaps were completely open and honest about how they carried out the hoax, describing in detail how, with the aid of a wooden plank and some string, they'd flattened the cereal crop into the unique patterns that became so familiar around the world. They did it, it seemed, solely for the sheer devilment. It took no more than my obvious sense of awe and a few pints of 6X to persuade them to give me a small demonstration.

They had created the world-famous elaborate circle patterns under cover of dark, of course. For me though, it was a demonstration in broad daylight. One guy stuck a stake with a very long piece of string attached into the ground between stalks of cereal in a large field no more than 100 yards from the pub. The outer end of the string held a large plank of wood, its narrow edge facing the central stake. The other chap took a crumpled piece of paper out of his pocket, briefly consulted it, then strode over to the plank and, by standing on it, pressed down the stalks. He repeated this action until it had described the perimeter of a large circle. Taking it in turns with the plank, they drew two such circles in a comparatively short time.

They explained that, even though we couldn't get an immediate birds eye view, they were confident that the pattern was faithful to their drawing and they'd inevitably get the media's 'attention. 'Aliens Visit Wiltshire Again' headlines would soon follow.

Back at the pub, and after another round of beers and packets of crisps, the older of the two told me that he'd got the idea years ago when he'd watched a report about the mystery of the Nazca Plain Lines on BBC2. The first circles had been hastily created in a field owned by his family. It'd roused such national (and, later, international) interest that the two of them sought out new, bigger agricultural canvases around their South West stomping ground.

I'm pretty certain that creepy folk stories such as 'The Devil's Footprints', and 'The Hairy Hands' (Both from

Devon, England) began in the same way as my do-it-yourself legend and the Crop Circle hoax. These two eerie inventions, supposedly first mentioned in print in the 1850s and 1940s respectively, are so well established as historic mysteries that few people, other than me, have bothered to check up on the authenticity of their sources. Both tales seem incredibly farfetched. One of them though has an explanation that's totally unexpected. Here are brief accounts of the legends.

It's the mid-19th century. One winter's morning, after a heavy snowfall, folk started reporting an unbroken trail of hooved footprints. Whatever, or whoever they belonged to was bipedal. They ran for many miles across counties in the South of England.

A hundred years later, during WW2, drivers started reporting the appearances in their vehicles of a pair of phantom hands that would grasp the wheel and try to steer them off the road.

Not only aren't there any reliable or verifiable first-hand accounts of these phenomena, but the source material is also distinctly dodgy. In both legends, no two eye-witness reports seem to agree.

The Devil's footprints are amazingly variable in location, shape, and size according to which report you read. The phantom hands that caused so many road accidents, are, in one telling, warm, hairy and strong, in another, skeletal and cold as ice. The hands are sometimes invisible and other times, terrifyingly visible. Surely, they can't all be the same phenomenon, can they?

Well, almost by sheer chance, I did unearth the truth of The Hairy Hands legend. Here it is:

The legend of The Hairy Hands began with two US soldiers, stationed in Devon, England, in pre-D-Day 1940s.They created, as a bit of giggle, what became an enduring Devon folklore tale.

I met one of these two rascals, Noah Smith, in London, in 1985. A native of Arizona, he was in his mid-60s then, but you could just tell by the gleam in his eye (and his capacity for downing pints) that the ol' mischief was still there. We were complete strangers, but our shared passion for beer, as it so often does, cut through any ice, and we chatted about all sorts of stuff. Naturally, his wartime service in England came up as a topic.

Back then, Noah and his buddy were vibrant young men, impatient and bored with all the waiting about between exercises, stuck in a very rural part of England that offered no worthy distractions.

One night, tipsy and careering around the windy little roads, at night, in a borrowed jeep, they'd come up with the crazy, spooky idea of a pair of ghostly hands that suddenly appeared in your vehicle and tried to wrench your wheel, causing you to lose control. This is where the story began.

It was, so I was told, just a bit of a drunken joke between the two young warriors, a kind of surreal excuse that they could give their superior officers for accidentally trashing a jeep. Of course, they got back to base unscathed, and never actually needed to use their bonkers excuse. The idea, it seems stayed with them though.

It inevitably got into the local papers. The sudden presence of so many US servicemen in a little out of the way country spot like that was a bit of a village sensation. Brought up, like the rest of the nation on the glamorous, exciting Hollywood images of North America, the local press, a callow youth, had been taken in, hook, line, and sinker, by the ghostly hands story told, with a straight face, by Noah himself.

It seems the two servicemen were both totally delighted and bemused by the way in which the story had grown over the years, into Devonian history. He said it was never their intention for that to happen. They really hadn't thought that far ahead. It was simply a bit of a lark for the two of them.

I've since learned that Noah's home state of Arizona has a couple of similar, although much older, ghost stories. Maybe one of those spinechillers helped stoke his creative genius that night?

So, how was it that I got to meet him in the first place? Did I arrange it? Was it a freaky coincidence? No. It's simply that until that chance meeting with Noah in a pub in Greenwich, I'd never heard of The Hairy Hands story. It was this encounter that roused my curiosity in the first place.

How did the ghostly yarn take off so quickly? Well, back in the late 1940s and early 50s, the newly laid Dartmoor Circular Rd, in particular, experienced a high number of accidents, sometimes several a week. I checked newspaper reports and magistrates' notes and records from that period. Quite a few of the car drivers placed the blame squarely on the non-existent shoulders of the ghostly hands. As I mentioned earlier, descriptions varied wildly.

I think there's a connection between a newly opened, freshly tarmacked stretch of road and an increase in faster driving. Increased speed vastly increases the likelihood of accidents. It's also extremely likely that sharing a bogus excuse, regardless of its bizarre nature, is a part of human nature. Teachers experience this phenomenon regularly.

If two or more students get away with something by using the same excuse, others will doubtless follow suit. It's unarguably a funny folk tale. It's also quite understandable how it managed to endure for nearly eighty years. As far as tourism in Devon is concerned, keeping the embers of this story aglow is essential. Devon has much to offer already: Beautiful countryside, wildlife, beaches, cream teas, historic sites. Another tourist lure can't do any harm.

Well, what about The Devil's Footprints then? It's a well-known tale. It's also one that, although extremely variable in its details, has held the world in thrall for over 170 years. Yet, there's one very big problem with the story.

In the mid-19th century, way before we had aircraft (and the views they offer) or phones for that matter, it was impossible to know the extent of the prints without our modern means of communication.

What about the newspaper stories of the time? To collect all the eye-witness reports from widely separate communities would take months, and a lot of expensive manpower. You couldn't simply tap a few keys on a PC, or smartphone. Yet, back then, almost immediately, the Devil's tracks were reported as extending across whole counties of England. The hoof marks even crossed estuaries, rivers, and scaled cliffs; it was said. How could anyone know all that? And know it so soon? The most obvious answer seems to be that the papers invented the whole thing. Why, though?

Other than the smattering of reports from The Crimean War, 1855 was, generally, a dull year for British news. A little supernatural titillation couldn't fail to grab the public's imagination.

That's a really important thing to think about when investigating these weird legends. Up until the last 100 years or so, we got our 'news' from papers, word-of-mouth, telegrams, and...well...little else. It was easier to plant the seeds of long-lasting urban legends back then than it is now. Much easier. Debunking myths and rumours can be almost instantaneous in the 21st century. In the mid-19th century, though, the majority of people really were more inclined to believe what they read in the papers.

Now, for example, the BBC's 'Reality Check' news service investigates the veracity of inflammatory claims made by high profile figures. The illegal use of dead electoral voters in the recent US election was debunked, as was the health dangers of vaccines, mobile 'phones, and, oh, I

17

don't know...jellybeans. All of these outrageous claims would have considerably longer shelf lives without our current technology.

So, the hoofed hoax started right at the moment some mid-19th century journo decided to launch it.

There are equally long-lasting legends that are based on true events. They've stuck around for so long because their disturbing origins have been mythologised. My job was to try and find some of the facts that preceded the myths. I was looking for hard evidence.

Mini nuns. Photograph taken in 1961 and given to Rosalind Heywood, a society for psychical research council member.

The hanging nun.
Photo credit: Duncan Robinson.

Ghostly Nuns Join the Picnic

The year was 1961. A teacher from a North Lincolnshire school snapped a picture of happy pupils enjoying a sunny picnic. They were seated at trestle tables. When the photos from that day were developed, the staff were astounded that, on one group shot, there was a procession of miniature ghostly nuns. I don't need to mention that nobody had noticed their presence at the picnic.

I'd first seen that creepy picture in 1993, in a magazine. I was flicking through it in my dentist's waiting room. I decided that, since next to nothing was known about the picture's origins, I'd investigate. I had just one tiny shred of a lead though. The accompanying text said the picture was taken near Brocklesbury, Lincolnshire. So, that's where I was going to go.

Twenty-four hours later, I'd checked my map, packed my bag, and was on the way to Grimsby. That famous port was my first call because that's where I'd find the main heritage centre, museums, libraries etc. After a leisurely drive, I booked into the beautiful Yarborough Hotel. Washed, changed, and fed, I headed out to do a bit of sleuthing.

Local Historian Margaret Ryle is certain that the picnic spot they chose was on the site of a 12th century Cistercian nunnery at Nun Cotham in Lincolnshire.

I met Margaret, an incredibly energetic and brilliant seventy-five-year-old, at The Heritage Centre. She worked there on a voluntary basis. Over coffee and cheese scones in the cafe, we discussed the infamous mini nuns' photo. She was a mine of useful information.

I learned that the habits they're wearing are remarkably similar to drawings of the costumes worn by Cistercian sisters of that period. They are quite distinctive outfits, with very full hoods, and quite unlike those of other orders.

She was confident that the nunnery at this location could well have been the first, and only Cistercian house in England at the time. She thought it was highly unlikely that anybody at the school would know that they were picnicking on the site of an ancient nunnery. The place had only recently been identified, and nobody outside the circle of a few eminent archaeologists would have heard it. Oh, and just to put the icing on the cake, Margaret knew which school the girls in the photo had attended.

I learned a lot more. Henry VIII had the nunnery dissolved in 1539. The earthworks remain though, as do evidence of barns and the ruins of a 17th century house. There are also two fishponds that are believed to be part of the old nunnery grounds. That particular part of Lincolnshire was no stranger to weird, spectral happenings, she told me.

Reports of ghostly figures go back many years. Periodically, throughout the 20th century, there were reports of an invisible drowning girl who splashed about in one of the ponds, screaming for someone to save her. Along with grey ladies, wailing child ghosts, and various spectral riders, there were a few poltergeist happenings.

The next day, in Grimsby Library, thanks to those trusty microfiche records, I found more sightings from local papers.

In 1927, The Malvern Journal reported that two farm workers had seen the body of a woman hanging from a tree near Roxton Wood, adjacent to the nunnery site. According to one of the men, when they approached the ghastly figure, she disappeared with a long-drawn-out sigh. Frustratingly, her costume is not described. That's a pity. I was really banking on it being a nun's habit, or, at the very least, a wimple.

My sketch of Nun Cotham Priory and surrounding area.

A peculiar sighting in 1950 tells of an abandoned phantom baby. Three children were playing near the old Cotham Manor one afternoon when they heard a baby crying in the ruins of the building. Unable to find the child, they ran home to their village, Limber, and told their parents. On investigation, a couple of the adults found only a dirty old swaddling blanket and a small crucifix on a chain.

Ah! A crucifix. That bucked me up alright. At least there was a religious connection.

The next item I found really got my attention though. It was dated Saturday 10th April 1937. Two people had, independently, reported seeing a lady in a black hood walking in Miller's Wood. Her outfit was described by both people as looking like a nun's robes. One said that her face was pretty, but very pale. The other witness said that she was crying. In both cases, the apparition was walking towards the viewer and faded quickly. Now, that's much more like it, I thought.

The black hood detail was particularly exciting. Cistercian nuns wore black hoods.

Miller's Wood practically borders on the old nunnery grounds. It's a stone's throw to the South West of the place. This was a real break in the case.

When carrying out preliminary tests on this site, archaeologists confirmed that the ground level of the Mediaeval nunnery (and its grounds) was about two and a half metres lower than today. It's pretty likely that these weren't tiny nun ghosts that had been photographed. They were just at a lower level than the picnickers. That didn't tie in with the Miller's Wood sightings though, I thought. Their nun figure was walking on the same level as themselves.

There was only one thing for it. I had to check out Miller's Wood. By now, I'd booked into a cosy hotel in Immingham, so the old nunnery grounds were about three miles away.

They served excellent local bitter at my hotel, so, after four of them, and an equally superb meal, I decided to delay my visit and have a lie in instead. So, on my third morning there, after a very light breakfast, I was off to the wood.

I had checked out a map of the area, printed in 1935. It showed a main path that crossed the wood, North to South. It was easy to find. I'd only taken twenty or so steps into the trees when I had the answer.

The path descended, steeply at first, then more gradually, to a dell. Spooky Nun had been ascending the path towards the witnesses. Unlike the mini nuns' picnic spot, the ground levels of the wood had remained pretty much the same over the last seven hundred years, or so. There had been successive layers of habitation on the nunnery grounds, but not here in Miller's Wood. I don't know why I hadn't thought of that before. Mediaeval feet had trodden the same wood path (or one very like it) as me.

A few hours later, back at my hotel, I got an amazing break. Chatting with the owner, over an early afternoon pint, I told her about my ghostly nun quest.

"Hold on", she instructed me. "I've got a book that'll interest you."

She left me sipping my bitter and popped behind the bar to retrieve it. I was all agog.

She placed in my eager hands a book called *Lincolnshire Legends and Lore,* and flicking it open, pointed to a black and white photograph. The caption told me it was taken in Brocklesbury Park in 1978 by A.E Horner. The park is right next to Nun Cotham, but it was the image that sent my pulse racing.

It was a pretty, atmospheric shot of a wooded clearing. To the left, though, in the mid distance, there seemed to be a figure hanging by its neck from a side branch of a tree. Looking closer, it was possible to make out a female form, dressed in robes with a full hood. A nun! Surely this had to be a nun.

This was excellent. My host brought me another pint and left me to study the text. It seemed that Horner hadn't noticed anything out of the ordinary in the picture until they'd developed it. It made me wonder if the photographer had returned to the spot to have another look Even a bit of tell-tale rope attached to the branch would have debunked the ghost idea.

Well, I'm not sure if it was the beer talking, but a little voice in my head told me to check it out for myself. How the heck could I figure out where the hanging tree was though? I decided to finish my pint, order sausages and chips for lunch and think it through.

Lincolnshire sausages are amazing though, and they had my full attention throughout the lunch. It was part way through my superb carrot pudding that it came to me. I could contact the publisher of *Lincolnshire Legends and Lore*, and ask them for A.E. Horner's telephone number, or, failing that, their address. Hopefully, he or she would remember roughly where they took their shot. I found it a bit weird that there was no mention of Horner's sex in the book.

I rang the publishers from the payphone in the lounge. Sadly, they only had a PO Box address in Bath for the photographer. I briefly thought about sending a letter, but I was planning on getting back to Leeds in a day or two, so it didn't seem worthwhile. Any attempt to find the tree by myself would be utterly pointless - like looking for a needle in a haystack. Instead, I asked my kind host if I could get a copy of the photograph. She happily agreed, wishing me luck with my quest.

The next day I was back off to Grimsby for two good reasons. Firstly, I was going to get a photocopy of the pic from a printer's shop, and secondly, I needed to consult that font of knowledge, Margaret Ryle.

She was as just as happy to meet up again as I was. Rather than simply barge in asking for information, I took her to lunch at The White Hart pub. I ordered beers and nabbed us a quiet corner table. We both had the delicious haslet salad, followed by Toad-in-the-hole (Those lovely sausages again), and Stilton on crackers. We washed them down with a glass of port each and got straight into the nun mystery.

I brought her up to speed with everything I'd discovered. Margaret already knew about the various ghost-nun sightings, both the hanging and walking varieties. I showed her my copy of the picture from the book.

After she'd studied it for a few seconds, a memory seemed to have popped into her head. Pushing the photo back across the table, she asked if I would pass her my Lincolnshire map. I was beginning to sense progress.

Margaret opened up the map, smoothed it down, briefly studied it, then jabbed her finger down on 'Barton Upon Humber'.

"This was once the Mediaeval borough of Barton", she announced. "There was a castle built here, during King Stephen's reign, in the 12th century. It was put up by Lord Gilbert de Ghant. Now, there was a scandal back then involving an extremely high-born unmarried lady, Agnes de Gril.

Agnes, a prominent member of his wife's inner circle, found herself pregnant. The father was known to be one of Gilbert's knights, William Alan. When it all came out, Agnes' family wanted her packed off to a Cistercian nunnery in France, either permanently, or at least until the dust had settled.

You see, they had her already lined up for marriage with a wealthy, titled French bloke. The Cistercian house was chosen because Agnes' parents had made generous donations to the place for many years. It would be practically the same as sending her off to hide away safely with family friends."

Margaret paused at this point, not for dramatic effect, but to take another sip of her port. I drained my glass in one gulp.

"Gilbert's good Lady-wife intervened on behalf of her friend. She asked if Agnes might be installed at an English nunnery instead. The reason she gave him was that Agnes was her closest friend and they couldn't bear to be parted.

Gilbert could not say no to his beloved wifey, so, as you've guessed, Agnes turned up at Nun Cotham, a mere twelve miles, or so, from Gilbert's castle. The genuine reason, however, was that the baby's knightly father was as deeply in love with Agnes as she was with him. Secret meetings had already been planned between the lovers.

The plan was for the baby to be born and raised at the nunnery and for Agnes and her knight to get together as often as humanly possible. At those times, it was usual for the other nuns to turn blind eyes to that sort of thing, especially when it involved rich patrons and their friends.

When Agnes was admitted, Lord Gilbert had been obliged to make some fitting donations to the place.

The cosy plan didn't work out, sadly. Less than a year later, tragedy washed away the lovers' hopes. Agnes' love, William was killed during one of the crusade campaigns. Driven mad with grief, Agnes wandered off and killed herself in the woods. It's not known exactly how she topped herself, but both drowning and hanging are mentioned in sources."

Margaret's encyclopaedic knowledge had come to my rescue. This was stunning. I had no doubt that, down the centuries, there had been many such tragic conclusions to forbidden love affairs. Agnes, though, had to be number one candidate for the position of hanging nun. Hold on though.

Wait a minute! Hadn't I read about a drowning woman ghost in the same area? No! Forget it, I reasoned. Throwing a drowning phantom nun into the mix at this stage would be madness.

The baby's fate wasn't known though. Margaret reckoned that, in keeping with Lordly custom, the child's upbringing would have been paid for by his Lordship. When he had come of age, he'd most probably be taken into his Lordship's service at the castle.

So, I had some answers at last. If there really were supernatural phenomena at Nun Cotham, poor Agnes would be right at the centre of them. There were, of course, loose ends, like the crying baby ghost, but, hey, you can't have everything.

I ordered two more ports. Margaret suggested that we'd be better off just asking for the bottle. We did. I then made two telephone calls, one to my Immingham hotel to cancel that night, and a second to The Yarborough to book in. There was no way I would be driving again that day.

Pixie hand, grub, or fungus?

A closer look.

Pixies and Elves. Solved!

Pixies and other tiny-folk sightings are still occasionally reported nowadays. Who knows what the witnesses have actually seen? Managing to photograph one is an even rarer occurrence.

The photograph at the beginning of this chapter was taken by a butterfly spotter in Essex. It first appeared in the July 2010 issue of *Mysterious English Countryside* magazine. When silently stalking a Large Skipper, he became aware of some movement in a nearby pile of dead wood. He instinctively swung his camera 'round and snapped a shot just as whatever it was disappeared from view behind an old log.

The resulting picture appears to show a tiny hand gripping the log as the creature swiftly lowered itself to the ground. Despite his efforts to grab another shot of the retreating thing, "it was just too damned fast", he said.

He did add that, from that briefest of glimpses, he could see a ping-pong ball sized head, topped by a shock of reddish hair. The face was pale and the features centralised.

The picture caused quite a stir when the July issue came out. I spoke to The Editor on the telephone. Like me, she thinks that the 'hand' could be a beetle grub, or, just as likely, Dead Man's Fingers' fungus. Still, it does make you look twice.

Where did the idea of pixies come from? I think there's a much simpler explanation than we might have expected.

Pixies are old. I mean, really ancient. Yes, they're definitely Cornish but, controversially, the name isn't. It's Irish.

Over a thousand years ago, Irish traders and settlers introduced the word, 'pixie' into the Cornish language. It was the abundance of tin, silver and copper that brought them to Cornwall. The Irish men referred to the small Cornish females as 'puca si', or she-spirits. 'Pixie' is a later mispronunciation, or derivation of that term. It was a sort of humorous nickname. 'Puca' meant spirit and 'si' was female.

A puca si, inspired by the Irish Aos Si Fairy folk.
Ironika/Shutterstock.com

You see, to the Irish men, Cornish women would be, noticeably, much smaller than their Irish counterparts. They were so struck by the delicate beauty of the young Cornish ladies that they compared them to faery folk.

The term, 'puca si' was a semi-joking name, drawn from the magical, aos si.

The aos si were, to the Irish, small supernatural beings. In folklore, they are described as, 'appearing amongst the living.' They came from an unseen world that coexisted with our own. In Gaelic art, the aos si are depicted as beautiful, ethereal females. They were fairies, petite and enchanting. It seems that the name stuck.

During the hundreds of years since, in popular mythology, pixies have transformed into a race - both male and female.

The ancestors of those Irish traders and settlers had arrived in Ireland a thousand years before Celts came there. Modern studies believe their ancestors had originated in The Middle East. Bones of an Irishman found in County Sligo, dating from 11th - 12th century, showed that he was 5ft 10in. Other ancient finds, of both sexes, in Ireland, indicate a much taller race of people than their neighbours across the sea.

What about elves then? Their first appearance in our cultures is even older than pixies. Originally, elves had only one function in folklore tales and it's from that role that we get the name, 'elf'.

All over Northern Europe there are ancient traditional stories of elves stealing healthy human babies. In many cases, the babies were replaced with their own elf babies. As they grew up, the imposter elf children often became sickly and less robust than human offspring, eventually dying. Infant mortality rates were much higher back then.

I think both the baby theft idea and the elf-human child swaps were methods of dealing with the traumas associated with these terrible losses.

The Latin word, 'elevo' meant to raise, take away, or reduce in worth. It's likely that this is where the words, 'elf', and its plural, 'elves' come from.

When the Romans arrived here in Britain, in 43AD, they brought with them a bunch of baby theft legends. There were babies that were abandoned in woods, stolen by demons, and, most famously, suckled by wolves.

You can bet your life that these Roman legends, along with the practical stuff, like roads and plumbing, were picked up by the Ancient Brits. Their conquered peoples took Roman gods, so why not also borrow their folklore yarns?

I think it's safe to say that pixies, fairies, gnomes, and the like are just fanciful names for people...you know...humans, like us. There isn't a single fossilised bone from any part of an elf. No leprechaun skeleton has been found. There's never been a single case of anyone trapping a fairy in a butterfly net. Even the famous Cottingley Fairies photos were faked. In our time, heat-sensitive cameras would have definitely picked up the tell-tale heat signatures of little folk flitting through the undergrowth.

Theses legends hark back to times when different tribes of people from geographically isolated places looked physically dissimilar from each other.

We know this from Mediaeval European accounts of first contacts with South American or African peoples. They are described and drawn as bizarre and unusual, perhaps as some might imagine extra- terrestrial aliens. Even as late as the 18th century, South sea islanders were viewed as strangely exotic and far removed from Europeans. In many cases, they were smaller as well. The fairy-tale little -folk of legend arose from unexpected encounters with peoples who were gob-smackingly different from the European explorers.

A first century AD Roman fresco (in the National Archaeological Museum, Naples) shows pygmies hunting Hippos on the Nile. The ancient Greeks and Romans wrote about tribes of pygmy hunters and farmers in Africa and Asia. Sometimes they are described riding on goats and attacking large birds that have invaded their crop fields. Other reports suggested they were magical beings, able to appear and disappear at will.

These accounts are from a time when Greek and Roman traders were regularly visiting the South West of England. Other peoples also enjoyed fruitful trading arrangements with British tribes. News of these stunningly exotic folk would inevitably lead to associations with magical powers.

What about leprechauns though? Where did they come from? There's no question about their Irishness, but, surprisingly, their origin are in Egypt.

To the ancient Egyptians, people with dwarfism were associated with the sun god Ra and given high positions in society. The god, Bes, is depicted as a dwarf. Paintings and statuettes honour them.

The Egyptians also believed that dwarfs carried good luck. That might very well be the origin of 'lucky' Irish leprechaun legends. Thousands of years ago, the ancestors of the Irish had lived in the Middle East. Figuratively speaking, that's right next door to Egypt. It's not hard to imagine them sharing some beliefs with their pyramid-building neighbours. And there's another striking connection between Bes and those leprechauns.

The Egyptian god, Bes.
Nick Brundle Photography/Shutterstock.com

The dwarf god, Bes' image has been found on numerous golden amulets, necklaces, pins, and other pieces from ancient Egypt. There's no doubt that gold was very much associated with the worship of Bes. All the jewellery found bearing Bes' face is wrought from gold. Irish leprechauns are said to possess gold; they jealously guard their crocks of the stuff, going to great lengths to hide it from the envious eyes of the big folk.

Looking at one example, an Egyptian amulet from between 664 and 332 BC, the face of Bes is surprisingly similar to that of the traditional leprechaun. In fact, most of these finds carry images that look a lot like the lucky little folk.

So, once again, there's a human origin for another race of the little folk. In this case, it's people with dwarfism. Ancient peoples, like the Egyptians, hadn't a clue about the actual causes of conditions such as this. To them, they were supernatural beings, powerful and esteemed.

It's only since trans-continental exploration opened up the world for travel that diverse groups mixed their genes. The more we mixed as a species, the less reports there were of supernatural little beings. In the same way, modern medicine allowed us to recognise the causes of conditions like dwarfism that made some people look a bit different from the majority. Travel and scientific understanding have gradually eroded the belief in elves, pixies, fairies, leprechauns, and the other fairy-tale little folk.

The Disappearing Toilet

I'd never heard of a ghostly toilet before. The idea of a phantom lav that randomly appears then disappears sounded to me more like something from a Terry Pratchett novel than the real world. Investigating this off-the-wall legend proved to be a genuinely weird experience.

I first heard of this phenomenon when staying with my cousins Patricia and Dave, in Aintree. We'd been close since we were kiddies and we often stayed with each other.

In those pre-marriage, pre-children days, the three of us had a lot of time on our hands. There was a lot of sessions in the pub, drinking beers and gassing on about this and that. Dave, it seemed, at that time, had a part-time job in Her Majesty's Civil Service in Bootle. He was based in a high-rise office block building called The Triad. It had twenty-three floors and Dave's filing duties found him on the ninth of these.

Not every floor had a Gents' toilet, so he when nature called, Dave would have to pop up one flight of stairs. In his first week in the place, he asked an older colleague where the loo was. The reply from the older bloke was puzzling. He advised Dave to use the Gents', two floors down instead of the tenth. It was more reliable, he said.

Now, Dave had naturally assumed that the lower loo would be preferable because the upper one was out of service or the plumbing was dodgy. As it turned out, that's not at all what he meant by less reliable. It was something altogether more outlandish.

After a gruelling morning's filing, tea drinking, and staring out of the window, Dave suddenly realised that his bladder was fit to burst. He decided to risk it and leg up the stairs to relieve himself. After a bit of a search along the long corridor, he located the loo. Whist washing his hands, he found himself wondering what could be the problem with the place? Everything seemed to work. It was well maintained and spotless.

It wasn't until four in the afternoon that he got the answer. Much coffee and tea were guzzled down in those days, especially at work. He went up a floor again to visit the lav. It had gone!

It's as simple as that. 'Confused' doesn't even come close to expressing Dave's state of mind. He wandered up and down the corridor. Nothing! Where the heck had it gone? There were offices, cleaners' cupboards, a copying room, and other spaces, but no Gents' toilet. Back down to the seventh floor he went. To his great relief, that loo remained.

It wasn't just Dave who'd had the ghostly experience though. Three of his fellow Clerical Assistants hadn't been able to locate the room that same day. Just to make things spookier, it had reappeared the next morning.
Dave talked to a chap from the wages office on floor ten. He'd worked there for three years and, according to Dave, he'd also been unable to find the loo the previous day. The Triad building was massive. I mean, absolutely huge. There seemed to be hundreds of rooms on each floor. In

those days, back in the 1970s, buildings of that size were not at all common in the North of England. Losing your sense of direction might be expected but losing a whole room?

The disappearance and subsequent appearance had happened just once. No doubt, with time, a weirdly spooky-ooky tale like this would grow out of control. In no time at all, the loo would be vanishing several times a day, reappearing in car parks, developing huge, Tardis-like, interior dimension, and...I don't know...flying or something.

Sitting there, in 'The Old Roan' pub, the three of us were perplexed. What was going on? I just had to investigate this. It was a Saturday. I asked Dave what the chances were of me visiting the building on Monday? He reckoned it wouldn't be a problem. He'd have to clear it with his boss though.

He did get the clearance. It seemed that his boss, Sue, had heard about the ghost lavatory phenomenon. In her view, anything that livened up their daily drudge had to be worthwhile. So, I was welcomed.

Two days later, I'd joined him for lunch in his canteen. After our faggots, chips, and peas, we were snooping 'round the tenth floor. Following a complete circuit, we'd established that the lav was exactly where it should be. By this time though, the supernatural toilet distraction had attracted a lot of attention. A bit of a crowd...well, about eight people had joined us on our detecting route. Dave had bigged me up as a sort of ghost investigator and his colleagues clearly expected results. The pressure was on.

I desperately needed a clue. Anything would do. As we passed a cleaners' cupboard, an idea popped into my overheated brain. I tried the handle. It was unlocked. I opened it, flicked on the light, and poked my head in.

There was a mop in a bucket, a broom, dustpan and brush, and, more interestingly, a large pull-along vacuum cleaner. It had a heavy, upright cylinder attached to a long hose. On the end of the hose was a wide mouthed nozzle. An idea was beginning to form.

Rubbing my chin theatrically, I stepped into the cupboard. This drew much muttering from the small group. I heaved the vacuum cleaner out into the corridor. It was a dead weight. I knelt down and peered under the drum-shaped cylinder. I could sense their curiosity building around me. The four rubber wheels were wide. There was very little ground clearance there. I turned to Dave.

"When does this corridor get cleaned?"

Dave just stared blankly at me. He obviously didn't have a clue, but a couple of eager hands shot up. Suddenly, I'd become a Primary School teacher. I selected one, the lady whose hand was up first. She was a team leader and knew the office routines well.

"Corridors are cleaned 'round sixish. It's less busy then. The loos are done twice a day."

"What times is this loo done?", I asked.

"They're all done just before lunch, at 12, and then between 6 and 7, after we've all gone home."

"Just before lunch", she'd said. Yeah. I remembered hearing the hum of a vacuum cleaner in the hall outside the canteen. I reckoned I had the solution.

I just needed to speak to the cleaner who cleaned floor 10 before I had the complete answer. Again, it was the team leader who gave me the information I needed. She informed me that Irene, the cleaner for that floor, had already done the loo before our arrival. I could find Irene on the ground floor, in the break room now. I thanked the team leader and headed down there.

I did promise our little group that, if they wanted to know where the loo went, they could join me and Dave for a few beers in the pub after work.

As it turned out, Irene was very helpful. What she told me explained the whole spooky-loo business. Neither she nor the other cleaners had heard anything about the disappearing toilet. In many workplaces, cleaners are not kept in the loop when it comes to information sharing. When I told her about the big fuss, she thought it was hilarious. She even asked if she could join us in the pub after her shift. Irene couldn't wait for me to do the big reveal. Also, she felt that I definitely owed her a drink.

At 6.30pm in The Jutland pub they had their longed-for solution. I was really enjoying being the showman. Patricia had also joined us, and, over beers and crisps, I laid the ghostly loo to rest.

In the day of its disappearing act Irene was cleaning the lav, as usual, at twelvish. The drag-along nature of the hefty vacuum cleaner made it cumbersome. The toilet door opened inwards, so when she'd finished, Irene had to open it, keep it ajar with her foot, and back out, dragging the vacuum after her into the corridor.

The door generally got a bit of a bashing when this happened. In doing so, the men's toilet sign had come loose and dropped to the floor inside the room. Irene hadn't noticed that at the time.

On my tour of the corridor earlier that day, I'd noticed that only the toilet, copying room, and big wigs' rooms had signs on them. All the other rooms were numbered, but unsigned. The metal name plaques were polished, rectangular, and glued onto the wooden doors. I'd fiddled with one of them in my tour. It was loose. Cheap glue, I thought.

Obliviously, Irene had dragged her vacuum cleaner over the sign. Being sticky side up, it had attached itself onto the underside of the vacuum. It'd most likely stuck to a wheel and somehow lodged under there.

So, into the cleaning cupboard went the loo sign, on the underside of her cleaner. It wasn't until much later in the day, about 6.30, that she found it. It was on the carpet in her cupboard where it had dropped off the machine. Naturally, she reattached it to the toilet door before entering for a second time.

And so, with scores of identical unsigned doors, our loo seemingly disappeared for six and a half hours. Magically, it was there again the next morning.

People don't bother committing to memory the position of a room if there's a sign on its door to tell them what's in it. On a corridor with hundreds of identical doors, what would be the point in that? Unless your room is directly opposite the Gents' or next door to it, you'd get into the daily habit of looking for the sign with, 'Men's Toilet' written on it.

How about the numbers then? Of course the doors are numbered, but, again, who would bother to memorise the number of the loo when it's got the description of the contents written on it? Anyway, even if a few anally retentive blokes did manage to locate the nameless toilet, they're not the ones who'd report it missing.

I was delighted with how well my explanation went down. There I was, lapping up all the attention. Looking back from now, I must have seemed a bit of a smug git. Who cares though? We all had a good laugh and plenty of beer.

Hang on! What about what Dave's older colleague had told him? He'd said that the seventh floor lav was more reliable. What did he mean by that? Had the tenth floor one disappeared before? And, if so, was it the same cleaner or a different one? Frustratingly, I never got any answers to that. It's way too late to tie up that particular loose end.

Finally, here's an alternative title for this chapter, suggested by my friend, Dawn Hiscock: 'The Disappearing Loo: To be read at your convenience'.

Silbury Hill. Solved!
Konmac/Shutterstock.com

West Kennet Long Barrow.
Awe Inspiring Images/ Shutterstock.com

Prehistory Mysteries: Silbury Hill and The Long Barrow Lights. Solved!

Silbury Hill, in Avebury, dates back to 2470 BC. It's an ancient puzzle that's baffled us for ages. What the heck was it built for? It seems to be a manmade hill. Why would prehistoric folk need another hill on the edge of downland? Was it a tomb? Nope! There's nothing inside it to suggest that. It's already been poked, prodded, x-rayed, and sampled. The hill is 120 feet high and 600 feet from side to side. Why build it?

The age-old problem is that archaeologists were wasting their time looking for some tangible evidence. It's what's missing from its Neolithic neighbour that gives us the true answer.

The hill took half a million tonnes of earth to make. That's long been known. More recently though, I've found out exactly what its purpose was. Silbury Hill is a prehistoric slag heap.

Archaeologists from The University of South Wessex carried out an experiment in 2003. I was one of the volunteer helpers. Using geophysical equipment and soil samples, they were able to find a pretty accurate figure for the total weight of earth dug out of the ancient ditches that surround Avebury Stone Circle. Half a million tonnes was the answer. That's not a coincidence.

The ditches date from the same time as the hill. The builders had to put the soil somewhere. It makes total sense.

Less than a mile away from Silbury Hill, there's a genuine mystery though. Kennet Long Barrow is a huge burial mound. It was constructed 5650 years ago and contained the remains of over forty people. There's no mystery about its purpose. It was a giant tomb. No. It's something altogether spookier that happens there.

The occasional appearances of weird green lights above the mound have mystified Wiltshire folk since the 18th century. They are always spotted after dark. Oh, and there's something else. Whenever they're seen, there is an unexpected death in the area. The death occurs within a two-mile radius of West Kennet Long Barrow.

Some of the local people who I've talked to believe the lights are a supernatural warning. The deaths, they think, mark an ancient sacrificial rite of some kind. Something lost in the mists of time. That might seem farfetched, but, as it turns out, there's something similar going on. Superstition plays a large part in this legend.

In 1991, twelve years before my amateur archaeological experience, I was staying in the pretty village of Avebury at my girlfriend, Jane's cottage. We'd met at college and, contrary to advice from friends and family, she had decided to put up with me. Jane was local to the area and happy to introduce me to the mysterious Neolithic places that surrounded her home.

One afternoon, when the two of us were picnicking next to the Long Barrow, she told me about the eerie green lights and their death-curse. So many sheep had popped their woollen socks. Even a few sheepdogs had croaked it after the lights had appeared.

I'm sorry. That was childish of me. I should have said up front that it was sheep. For generations, local landowners had found the corpses of animals that only the day before had been perfectly healthy.

Jane knew me well. She knew I'd want to get to the bottom of this legend. That would mean sticking 'round there for a while. She'd been hinting about us attending her best friend's wedding in Bath. The event was two weeks away.

I was pretty cold about the idea; I hated weddings almost as much as I hated funerals. They both depressed the heck out of me. Having said that, she probably knew I'd give in anyway and agree. I think she just wanted me to have another project that we could share in the meantime. It wouldn't be the first time we'd had fun looking into oldie time mumbo jumbo. In this case though, it turned out to be something shockingly real and human that was behind the mystery.

England is blessed with many great pubs, but there are few more welcoming than The Red Lion at Avebury. Not only is it the only pub in the world that has been built inside a prehistoric monument, but it's also a great place to pick up bits and pieces of legends and the like.

In the summer season, the place is jam packed with hippies, hikers, bikers, tourists and, more importantly for me, knowledgeable locals. Jane was brought up 'round there so she knew exactly the folk who could fill me in on the background to this weird legend. She made sure I got to meet a few.

Husband and wife, Clive and Valerie Bough were in their mid-70's. They were family friends of Jane and they'd lived in the village for decades. Clive shared my loves for beer and local history. Valerie and Jane shared the capacity for endless patience when it came to their blokes.

Clive had been born locally and his parents had grown up hearing stories about the green lights. According to Clive just about everyone, from Marlborough to Chippenham had a relative or friend who knew someone that had seen the portentous lights. Both he and Valerie had also spoken to local farmers who'd lost livestock on the same nights that they'd appeared.

For the next few days, our idyllic pub lunching, picnicking, countryside wandering routine brought Jane and I into contact with quite a few local folk. It became increasingly clear that all the eye-witness accounts were second or, more frequently, third hand. There was one guy though a farmer, who had something very interesting to say.

His name was Chris Chapman - Dennis. One early October morning, ten years earlier, he'd been checking on his flock in the lower field. It'd been an icy night and a frosty start to the day, so he wanted to see if they were all OK. He found a dead sheep against a hedge. He had naturally assumed that she'd been a bit dodgy and succumbed to the cold night. When he told his neighbouring farmer, he got a bit of a surprise.

His fellow sheep-keeper had seen twinkling green lights in the sky during the night. He had been walking with his dog near the Long Barrow at the time. Hmmm? A possible lead?

I asked him if he happened to remember the date this had happened. By chance, he did. It was the morning of 10th October 1981. He remembered because it was his birthday. It was Jane that had the presence of mind to ask him the question that didn't occur to me at the time.

"Has that happened before? I mean, have you found a dead sheep in the morning?"

Well, it turned out that, according to Chris, it wasn't uncommon for sheep to die from cold, disease pregnancy, and other factors. Lamb losses were also frequent. Checking up on this later, I learned that it's as many as one in 20 that perish.

It suddenly hit me. Farmer Chris hadn't been surprised, or even intrigued, by the sudden death. It was the fact that it occurred the same night as those lights were reported. As far as I could figure, down the years, local folk had been struck by the timing of the deaths, not the actual deaths themselves. I could almost hear some old crone's warning.

"Green light - Death tonight."

Old country sayings like that rhyme, so they must be true. Joking apart, I was starting to put together a solution to this old mystery.

Over a delicious Ploughman's Lunch and a couple of pints, Chris told us more. He was the third generation of folk to keep sheep there. He remembered his grandpa and his dad telling him about the Long Barrow lights. Both men had passed away by that time, so I couldn't ask them anything. It didn't matter. An answer was gradually emerging.

The next morning, we were in Devizes, the capital of beautiful Wiltshire. There, in the County Library, Jane and I consulted two works: *The Wiltshire Agricultural Gazette* and *Wonders of Weather* by John Dick. I had a copy of Dick's book back in Leeds and I remembered a particular section that dealt with unusual weather phenomena. Between us, after a few absorbing hours, we found what we were looking for. First, there was something from *Wonders of Weather*.

From 1771 to 1813, in his diary, Thomas Hughes of Stroud mentioned over 70 appearances of The Aurora Borealis. Also known as 'The Northern Lights', they would have been seen from Wiltshire. In those pre-light pollution days, you could imagine just how bright, how clear they would have appeared.

Back then, few folk, especially country dwellers, would have heard of electrically charged particles from the sun interacting with the earth's magnetic poles. They'd just see them as funny- looking lights.

Around that time, there were also sightings from elsewhere in The West Country. In February 1755 and on 22nd October 1788, the light show was particularly spectacular. A study of *The Wiltshire Agricultural Gazette* records gave us a curious connection.

There was a devastating outbreak of Scrapie in 1755 and a lesser one in 1788. It hit the West Country particularly hard. Thousands of sheep died. It wasn't known to be a transmissible disease until the 1930s, so its origin was open to speculation, especially of the mumbo jumbo kind. Those dates leapt off the page.

We seemed to have found a link between the sudden death of livestock on a large scale and the appearances of those mysterious shimmering lights. Was it as simple as that? A long-lasting association between the two things had survived into our more science-savvy age?

Why Kennet Long Barrow though? Jane reckoned that the local folk already knew the purpose of the barrow; it was an ancient burial mound. The old tomb had an association with death and the supernatural. That was already deeply instilled in the population, way before the green lights started. The Long Barrow itself was in a field grazed by sheep. It seemed quite reasonable that any weird lights seen in its vicinity would be identified as a portent of death. The deceased animals didn't even need to be near the spooky mound. They could snuff it just about anywhere within spitting distance for it to be viewed as ominous.

We both wondered why late 20th century farmers, like Chris' neighbour, didn't know it was the Aurora Borealis they had spotted? The answer to that was also in Dick's book. The further South they appear in England, the damper the air. They look more like sporadic, shimmering lights than the spectacular curtains seen further North.

Oh, by the way, on the night of 9th October 1981, Aurora Borealis was seen from quite a few locations in The West Country. That tied in nicely with Chris' tale. Mystery solved.

Despite my reluctance to attend, the wedding turned out to be a lot of fun. There was a free bar and a glorious buffet. They had cold crab cakes, turkey and cranberry sandwiches, and satay chicken on skewers. Jane even persuaded me to dance.

I definitely got a bit tiddly. I don't know if it was the food, the 6X, or the success of our investigation, but, in my elevated mood, I suggested to Jane that we should move in together. I had no clear plan in mind. I hadn't even thought about where we'd live - if it'd be Leeds or Avebury? I was clearly acting on impulse. Ever the patient partner, Jane just shrugged and suggested that I'd had enough beer and should get some sleep.

In hindsight, I'd massively overestimated my importance in her life.

The next morning, completely sober and aware of what a dickhead I was the night before, I headed off back home. A few days later, I got the 'Dear John' letter that I so richly deserved.

Neolithic nonsense

As a bonus, here are six things that I've learned from talking to proper archaeologists:

There is no evidence whatsoever that any of Britain's Neolithic constructions were connected with spiritual matters. Neither is there anything to suggest that ancient standing stone circles were used as astronomical calendars.

If you choose the right spot to stand, just about anything can be aligned with anything else. The rising midsummer sun is always going to shine directly through, or from behind, part of any structure, ancient or modern. It just depends on where you've chosen to stand.

Water systems, such as streams, brooks, rivers, or their sources were never considered holy or mystical. Of course water was important, but that doesn't make it sacred.

Commemorating your dead doesn't necessarily mean you have any religious beliefs. Just as many atheists do this. It's likely that they always did

Dancing was for fun, not part of any ancient fertility 'rites'. Be wary of any explanation that includes the words, 'fertility', 'harvest', or 'ritual'. These words are a sure sign that the speaker is simply guessing.

It's highly unlikely that these ancient folk would spend so much energy and resources on building things that gave them no practical benefits or even entertainment.

The Phantom Lollipop Lady

She appeared to the occasional unlucky passenger on the bus route between Aintree and Liverpool city centre. It was always after dark and, every time, at the same point on the route. Crucially, to have seen her, you must've been sitting on the upper deck.

I've chatted with one of the passengers who had seen her. She was grinning at him through the window, tapping her metal lollipop on the glass. Now, that doesn't sound so scary, does it? Remember that he was sitting UPSTAIRS on a double decker bus.

I should explain that, in England, Lollipop Ladies are road crossing guards, responsible for stopping traffic to allow children to cross at designated points.

Paul Rowney was on his way home from work when it happened to him. It was 1979, and Paul, knackered after a long shift at the bakery, had drifted off. His head resting against the gently vibrating glass, Paul was suddenly awoken by a sharp rapping on the windowpane. Raising his head and opening his eyes, he was shocked to see a long, pale, much-wrinkled face grinning at him. She wore the traditional cap and white coat of her trade. She held a black and white striped pole with a circle of metal attached to the top. It was with this that she'd tapped the window and awakened Paul from his slumber.

Paul told me that, for a second or two, he was disorientated. He assumed that an ordinary, everyday

Traffic Control Officer had spotted him snoozing when the bus had stopped in traffic.

It was just as the bus started to move again that he remembered that he was on the upper deck. He looked back to see if he could still see the lady, but she'd disappeared.

Now, another creepy thing about this apparition is that some witnesses think she was a giant figure, easily as tall as a double decker. Others thought she was floating above the street level. Nobody, it seems, had looked down to see which of these things were the case. I can't blame them. The sudden appearance of that long wrinkly face gurning at me would get 100% of my attention.

In 1999, during a stay with my cousins in Liverpool, I checked through some newspaper articles. The Liverpool Record Office at the Central Library is on the awe-inspiring William Brown Street. They hold thousands of microfilm articles.

It was my cousin, Patricia, who'd introduced me to this ghoulish story and recommended The Records Office. We'd been close pals since we were toddlers. She lived, with her older brother, David, in a house on the haunted bus route itself. In fact, the spot where the lady appears is directly opposite their row of houses at an area called 'The Old Roan' in Aintree itself.

The records told me that there's been about twenty eye-witness accounts of the phenomenon. Some are quite detailed, others less so. All of them indicate the same location, at a set of traffic lights near 'The Old Roan pub.

The first mention was from 1960. The latest was from 1989. Nothing since then. Has she decided to retire from the haunting business?

In all but one sighting, she appeared to one passenger. It was always a male, and, in every case, he was snoozing. The exception was in 1970. A bus conductor also saw the lady as he entered the top deck to check tickets. Again, it was a male though, not a clippy. The conductor's account backed up that of one of his fairs, a chap who'd just been rudely 'woken by the scary Lollipop Lady. Both said she was impossibly tall and vanished when the bus started moving again.

I got to meet Paul Rowney in The Old Roan pub. He was sixty-four at the time. The excellent old inn is just a short walk from Patricia's place. It was one of the two reasons that she chose to buy the house. The nearby train station was the other lure.

When I contacted them, the newspaper office was happy to give me the contact details for two of the ghost eyewitnesses. Paul was one of them. He lived in Aintree, so we arranged to meet up.

It was a beautiful sunny summer's evening, so we sat outside sipping our beers. Paul pointed out the exact spot where she'd appeared. Back then, when he saw her, he was due to get off the bus at the next stop. He joked that he wanted to thank her for waking him up. He would've missed it otherwise.

He had that typical Scouser's wit, the ability to find humour in just about any situation. Like me, he also liked a few beers in friendly places like The Old Roan. He struck me as a down-to-earth chap. His recounting of the event had the ring of truth about it. His honest nature was further strengthened by his insistence that he matched me round for round at the bar. He seemed just as keen as I to get to the bottom of this mystery.

There was one detail that Paul told me that hadn't appeared in any of the articles though. It set me thinking.

Paul said she had worn the older cap. It was an all-black, peaked one, with a green badge attached to it. She also wore a white coat and not the yellow high visibility one worn from the early 80s. If she was the restless, or simply mischievous, spirit of a dead person, details like this would help me find who she was.

I asked Paul to draw a sketch for me. With only a biro and my notepad, he drew a very detailed one; he'd even noted down the colours of the cap badge and the lollypop disc. Her circle, atop the black and white striped pole, had STOP in black letters on a red background. Her green metal cap badge also turned out to be a vital clue to her origins.

These extra clues pointed me towards a possible candidate for the ghostly lady. I followed up that enjoyable meeting with Paul with a visit to the local council offices. A patient bloke there gave me the connections I needed. He showed me detailed charts and lists of uniforms, badges, and the like that had been issued to Council employees down the years. Those particular red-faced lollipops were used between 1955 and 1965. They were replaced by white discs with orange bands below and above the STOP. The cap badge was more interesting though.

The distinctive green metal version was used in conjunction with the red disc between 57 and 60. For just three years. Whatever befell our phantom lady, it had to have happened in that period.

Cousin Patricia had a personal computer. It was one of those big creamy coloured boxy things that took about a day to connect to anything. She let me use it. Previously, I had only ever used a computer for word processing my textbooks. Oh, and for playing 'Sam and Max' and 'Day of the Tentacle'.

Computers had seriously speeded up the whole writing thing for me, but I was bloody hopeless at accessing anything else it offered. I did, however, after much finger-drumming, discover that Ribble double decker buses stopped running in 1989. They were the only two-storied buses on the Aintree route. Hmmm? Wasn't that just about the same time that sightings of our Lollipop wielding ghost stopped?

It was Patricia who nudged me in the right direction. It was during a memorable dinner at The Old Roan. Her, Dave, and I had Whitebait, followed by Lancashire Hotpot and, to finish, Bread and Butter Pudding. Hell's Bells! We could hardly cram down the cheese and port after all that. During our after-meal Drambuies, she said, "Do you think the Lollipop Lady was run over?"

Wow! I hadn't thought of that. That was certainly an occupational hazard for a Lollipop Lady. I decided, then and there, to check out any road accidents between 1957 and 1960 in The Old Roan area.

The next day, again, I found myself at The Records Office, trawling through microfilm. Nothing for 57, 58, or 59, but, sure enough, on Wednesday, 16th November 1960, there was a recording of a traffic accident at The Old Roan, Aintree, that matched.

Her name was Madeleine Windsor, aged fifty-eight. She was the victim of a hit-and-run. It happened at 4.30 PM, and in full view of some school children. She was a crossing guard. One witness, a taxi driver, had seen a car swerving, out of control.

Another horrified onlooker said that driver was slumped forward at the wheel as if asleep.

Mrs Windsor had been standing in the road, presumably to direct a group of kids across the busy road, with her back to the car. After the car had mowed her down, it continued its erratic course for about 50 yards. The dozing driver must have woken up at that point because the vehicle came to a stop. As several adults rushed to Mrs Windsor, the driver restarted his car, and sped off. The Lollipop Lady died in an ambulance on the way to Hospital.

This was way before CCTV, so finding the offender was a tough ask, even with descriptions given at the scene. Despite that, the car was traced.

Getting hold of an old Police Accident Report wasn't at all straightforward. I sent a handwritten letter to the Police Headquarters explaining my interest in the incident. I enclosed the fee, a £15 cheque. By the time I had a reply, it was three weeks later, and I was back home in Leeds. I'd sort of guessed it would be a bit of a wait, so I'd given my Headingley Lane address.

Seven witnesses were interviewed at the scene. It being an ordinary working day, there were fewer adults about. I'm not sure why, but none of the children gave statements.

One of the seven adults had a better view of the accident than the other six. He was a top deck passenger in a bus which had stopped at a set of lights. He was able to identify the make and model of the car. Vitally though, he saw and remembered the registration number.

The light blue Austin Cambridge and its owner were located. Of course, the copy of the report I'd received gave no more information about the killer.

It sort of fitted together. I wondered if Madeleine's restless shade revisited the fateful scene for two reasons. She might well have been waking the occasional bloke who'd nodded off on the upper deck because, well, he might miss witnessing an accident. Another, less clear, reason might be that it was a sleeping chap who'd run into her.

Whatever it was that drew her spirit back, she appeared to be a gently mischievous presence. There was no wailing and bemoaning from her ghost. And when the double decker stopped appearing on the route, so did she.

After closing the book on this case, I was still left with an unanswered question. During our chat, Paul had failed to mention his eight-year prison sentence, from 1960 to '68.

I know his personal life was none of my concern, but, after reading the accident report, it made me wonder. Twenty years after my Liverpool investigation, I found 'The UK Prison Database' online. I just had a hunch that something wasn't quite right about Paul's account. In Hindsight, it seemed strange to me that he could recall so much detail about the ghost.

Other witnesses gave the barest outline of her appearance. It was almost as if he'd done research of his own, perhaps in a bid to get some kind of closure.

'The UK Prison Database' came up trumps. There he was. He'd done his stint for failing to stop, leaving the scene of a fatal accident, and causing death. He was released on 21st September in 1968. I think he had agreed to meet me because he was seeking some kind of closure, a way to come to terms with it. He was never going to own up to me about his crime. Somehow, though, pretending that he'd seen her ghost may have helped him deal with the guilt. Who knows?

I can't leave it there without saying a bit about Madeleine (Maddie). She contracted and recovered from polio when she was a teenager, got married in 1927, had three children, and served as a military nurse in WW2. Her husband, Rob, was a marine engineer who joined the Merchant Navy during the war and survived her by fifteen years. She was born and lived her entire life in the Liverpool area.

She loved film musicals and Judy Garland was her favourite performer. Her preferred drink was a ruby port, and she was partial to vanilla ice-cream. Dressmaking and crosswords were her main pastimes. She also collected donations for the Leonard Cheshire Homes charity.

It's only since things like the internet and social media came along that I've been able to discover anything at all about her. Actually swapping emails and messages with members of her family really helped to paint a picture of Maddie.

Figure? An unused photograph from English County Lives magazine.

The Ghost of Cassiobury Park

I'd heard about the ghost of Cassiobury Park in 1985. I was researching various spooky things in the south east at the time. It was from my landlord, Mr Ugric, that I learnt about the ghost of a Civil War soldier who, on particular nights, hung about in the parkland behind Cassiobury Park Avenue. Well, my comfortable rented room looked out over that park. Fortunately, I'd chosen a good spot for ghost-watching.

I had a few things to check out in The British Library and The Public Records Office in London that week. I decided to have a snoop 'round Cassiobury Park House too.
I wish I'd asked Mr Ugric for more details. It turned out that the house had been demolished in the 1920s. That would explain why the ghost hangs out in the park instead. I headed straight for the library to check out any records. After a thoroughly absorbing afternoon, I had plenty.

It seemed that Lord Arthur Capel of Cassiobury House and Hadham Hall was a Royalist during the Civil War. He was executed in 1649. It was reported that, after his death, his heart was ripped out, placed in a box, and buried in the park. It's supposed that his restless shade is searching for that hidden ticker. The legend of his haunting is so strong that, even today, paranormal societies meet in the park every march, to try and spot his troubled spirit.

Incidentally, nearly thirty years after my visit, the 'Watford Observer' newspaper reported a particularly convincing sighting in March 2014. The accompanying photograph, taken by a member of Watford Paranormal Group, shows a swirling misty vision. It's a chilling shot. The more you stare at it, the more the mist seems to take on human forms. There are faces emerging from the fog. It's definitely worth checking out.

Back then though, buoyed by my finds, I asked one of the librarians if there was any other place that I might find info on the haunting. She was only too pleased to help. She headed off to a long row of drawers, slid one open, riffled through it, withdrew a file, and returned. I could tell by her smile that she knew I wouldn't be disappointed.

The file contained a series of photographs that were said to have been taken for *English County Lives* magazine in 1925. That was just two years before Cassiobury House was destroyed.

There were the usual interior shots of opulent rooms and impressive gardens. The particular photo that stood out was, for obvious reasons, not printed in the final magazine spread.

Looking at it sent a chill right up my spine. I'm sorry for the banality, but there's no other way of describing the effect it had on me. It was a picture of a well-ordered, spacious library. Although there were no people in the photo, an uninvited spirit guest had materialised.

There could be no mistake. In a corner of the room, a ghostly figure had taken shape. Something or someone had appeared.

I asked the helpful librarian where these pics had come from. It seemed that the offices of the now defunct *English County Lives* magazine were in the same building as the library. Struggling to compete with the deluge of gossip mags that hit the stands in the 50s, the publication had folded.

Quite a lot of paperwork and pictures were just left in the building. The majority of the stuff went the way of the dustbin lorry. However, according to the librarian, one of her predecessors had the wit to stash away a few interesting bits and pieces.

My host left me to return to her duties; libraries were very busy places back then. I turned the photo over. There was a handwritten note: 9th March 1925. Library. Figure?

The ceiling lights were off, and the daylight was coming from behind and to the left of the photographer. It was taken during the day. I couldn't really give a rough estimate of the time of day though.

'Figure?' That was the only comment from the editor who'd examined it. Clearly, the magazine had only one agenda. If they weren't tasteful portraits of nice gardens or elegantly arranged rooms then they'd ditch the shots.

I asked if I could use their coin operated machine to make myself a copy of the photo. She said I could have the original. Thanking her profusely, I grabbed my prize, and left.

The more I looked at it, the more I wondered. Was that his Lordship's ghost? Could it be a different spirit?

I needed a plan. I also needed a beer and a snack. On my way back to my room, I stopped off for a pint and a cold beef sandwich in a lovely pub called, I think, 'The Crown'. I might have got that name wrong. Either way, it was on The High Street and offered me a friendly, comfy space to gather my thoughts.

One pint of bitter led to another and, after a couple of hours' musings, I had made a decision.

First, after dark, I was going to check out the haunted park. Secondly, the next day, I'd get hold of a magnifying glass and have a closer squint at the photo's ghostly intruder.

After a lovely supper with my hosts, Mr, and Mrs Ugric, I headed for Cassiobury Park. Mrs Ugric was an ace cook. Her Chicken Paprikash followed by Kifli really hit the spot. I was well fed and ready for anything the 'other side' might send.

It was around 9.30, after a pleasant stroll 'round the vast parkland, that I came across a group of paranormal enthusiasts. The five of them had set up some equipment in a quiet, bushy corner. I asked them what they were doing.

One of the group, Olivia, a smiley middle-aged lady, explained the ins and outs of the box of tricks they'd mounted on a tripod. It contained a highly sensitive microphone that could pick up sounds that humans can't detect. There was also a special camera, the explanation of which involved so many words I didn't understand, I completely tuned out. They were very well prepared.

I found out that they were there to try and get a glimpse of Lord Arthur Capel. It was early March and, according to tradition, that was when his phantom form roamed the park in search of his buried heart. I told them that I was investigating His Lordship's spirit. They crowded 'round as I took out my copy of the ghost photo.

This definitely got their interest. They passed the photo between themselves. It was, once again, Olivia that spoke.

"That's definitely not Lord Arthur's ghost. It's got one head too many. He had his removed".

Ah. I hadn't thought of that. I suppose I should have realised it would have been the chop for the old Royalist. They were a very knowledgeable group, and it was another of them, a youngish bloke called Nick, who filled me in on the supernatural history of the park.

It was believed that, prior to the 12th century market settlement, this place had been largely common land. Strangely though, the local people tended not to use it for grazing or gathering wood or fruits. Why avoid all that freely given stuff?

From as early as the 17th century, there have been finds of human and animal bones, and weapons. This seemed to be a place of sacrifices dating back over two thousand years. He told me that local museums had a number of artifacts of this nature on display.

There were grisly looking blades, deeply scored bones, cloven skulls, and strangely marked amulets. It was small wonder that the local folk, with their deep-rooted beliefs in supernatural forces, gave the area a wide berth.
So, in all likelihood, the phantom photo-bomber could be the spirit of one of those ancient victims. Judging by the number of bones and stuff that had been unearthed here over the centuries, identifying this ghost would be like looking for a needle in a haystack.

So that settled it. I'd put this case to bed, and, in the morning, I would head off to London to do some other research. In the meantime, my five new acquaintances suggested I join them at their vigil. A couple of hours later they'd brought out the beer cans and we were happily swapping supernatural stories and toasting each other's health. No guest appearance by His Lordship though. Not to worry. I'd made some new friends who shared my interest in weird stuff.

In the wee small hours, after we'd exchanged contact details, I headed off back to my digs with a spring in my step. It was uplifting to meet fellow investigators who, like me, were just as happy to debunk something as they were to find evidence for it. I'd made up my mind to have the ghost photograph looked at more closely when I was in London.

The next afternoon found me on Brick Lane, in a shop called Montgomerie's Cameras and Lenses. I'd read about them in a copy of *Folklore Investigator* magazine. They were the photo experts that had first cast doubts on The Cottingley Fairies images in the early 1920s. If you had a mysterious photograph and you wanted in checking out, they were the world's best.

One of the staff, Stephen, was only too happy to have a squint at the ghostly intruder shot. He brought out a peculiar looking instrument and placed it on the countertop. It was a vertically elongated wooden box, about a foot high, open at the top, and of matt black metal. It bore a silver plaque that told me it was made by, 'Charles Frank Ltd, Glasgow'.

Stephen uncoiled a cable from its side and plugged it into a counter-top socket. I could see the box's internal lights reflected in his glasses as he leaned over to have a peek inside.

Attached to the rim of its open top were four lenses of different widths and thicknesses. He took the photo, slid it into a horizontal slot at the bottom of the box and then, peering down through one of the lenses, wound a little wheel, positioned just above the slot. I guessed that this would raise and lower the platform on which he'd positioned the photo, enabling Stephen to zoom in and out.

After about five minutes scrutinizing with the four lenses, Stephen broke the silence.

"Whatever this is was definitely in the room when the photo was taken."

This sounded promising. He lifted the photo out and slid it across the counter to me.

"It's either a trick of the light or this thing was in the corner of the room. There doesn't seem to be any photo fakery here."

So, there were three possible explanations:

1. It was a trick of the light.
2. A full-sized fake ghost was placed in the room before the photo was taken.
3. A real ghost paid a visit to the room.

I thanked Stephen profusely and headed to a pub to gather my thoughts. Two bitters later, in the beautiful old Prospect Of Whitby, I'd eliminated explanation number 2 from my list. It seemed daft to go to all the trouble of constructing a fake life-sized (Or death-sized?) figure in the room when the photograph was going to be rejected. Anyway, for *English County Lives* magazine, ghosts were definitely not allowed.

The more I looked at the figure, the less it looked like something to do with the light. A reflection of some kind was a possibility, I suppose, but a reflection of what? And, come to think of it, what was it reflected in? It just looked too 3D for a that. Also, there was something that looked vaguely like a face, partly obscured by the mantelpiece.

After another half pint and a delicious steak and kidney pudding, I decided that if there was ever a good candidate for a real ghost, this was it. I might not have found the Cassiobury Park spirit, but here was something truly uncanny.

It's thirty-five years later and nobody's offered a tangible explanation for the uninvited ghostly guest in the photograph. I reckon that, often, it's even more satisfying not to have a definitive answer to some things. There's a lot of stuff that's just a bit out of reach of our current understanding. Not knowing exactly what something is doesn't seem to deter people like quantum physicists.

They just keep on digging up pieces of the jigsaw, painstakingly building up the picture. To them, the bits that are missing are even more exciting than the ones they're found.

I loved my stay in Watford and I've been back there quite a few times over the decades. I kept in touch with Mr and Mrs Ugric for many years and I always stayed with them when I was in their lovely neck of the woods. The lure of her incredible Hungarian cooking was enough of a draw on its own.

Her name was Karole. She used to joke that when she died, she was going to come back as a ghost and haunt the heck out of me; that'd really give me something to investigate. She added that, if I went first, she would charge my ghost a nominal rent for the room.

I was a guest at the weddings of both their daughters, got drunk at their 50th wedding anniversary, and, lastly, attended their funerals. Joszef survived Karole by six months. He probably couldn't bear to be without her.

Cinderella's Slippery Lips and Fairy-tale Fibs.

As a story, Cinderella doesn't make much sense. I had to answer three puzzling questions before I could figure out what is really going on in this classic German tale:

Why does her glass slipper remain glass after midnight?

Why would anyone wear a glass slipper in the first place?

Why don't her ugly sisters and stepmother recognise her at the ball?

Glass? The mystery of why it appears to be a uniquely impractical piece of footwear was solved when I heard another German fairy tale. The key word in that last sentence is, 'heard'.

Three years ago, I was on holiday in Austria with my wife, Lizzy, and our two children. In between sight-seeing, walking, eating, and drinking, we opted to laze about in our chalet watching TV.

I watched a kid's show featuring a cartoon version of 'The Princess and The Frog'. The narration was, as you'd imagine, in German. At the crucial moment when the kind princess kisses the froggy, the narrator describes her as having a pair of smooth lips. In German, that's: 'Ein paar glatte lippen'.

Spoken aloud, to an English speaker, that sounds a lot like, 'A pair of glass slippers'.

A long time ago, some non-German speaker heard the story of Cinderella read aloud. He or she misinterpreted a similar description of Cinder's lovely lips. Her pair of smooth lips (Glatte lippen) makes such more sense than glass footwear.

It's easier to imagine the Prince touring his land, kissing every girl who might prove to be his mystery date. This is much more plausible than the idea that Cinderella is the only girl in the entire kingdom with that particular shoe size. That's just plain stupid, even for a children's tale.

Yes, but why go through the whole kiss test thing? Why wouldn't he just recognise her face? Come to think of it, why didn't Cinderella's ugly sisters and wicked stepmother recognise her at the ball?

It was a masked ball. The Prince, her step mum and stepsisters wouldn't have seen her face that night. The earliest illustrations of the story depict the ball guests wearing masks that cover their noses and eyes. So, no slippers, glass or otherwise played a part in the original version.

It shouldn't surprise us too much that a kiss is involved. The kiss has always been a type of magic trigger in stories.

Sleeping Beauty and Snow White are both revived from death-like slumbers by a kiss. Our prince-frog hero is restored to his human shape by a timely smacker. When Beauty finally sucks face with The Beast, he turns back into a handsome bloke. I suppose we're meant to forgive him then for kidnapping the girl in the first place.

This whole Cinderella business got me thinking about how these fairy stories started. Who invented all those talking wolves, wicked witches, and mischievous elves? How did weirdy little sadists like Rumpelstiltskin emerge? It was women. Women invented them all. And they had a bloody good reason for doing so.

Women invented wicked witches and wolves

Most of the fairy tales we're familiar with today grew out of a parent's need to scare their little darlings into putting safety first. The Big Bad Wolf, Rumpelstiltskin, witches, The Pied Piper, ogres, and scary goblins are all assumed to be imaginary figures. They popped up in various traditional tales hundreds of years ago, in a Europe beset with dangers.

Plagues, wars, wild animals, slave traders, kidnappers — every manner of evil threatened to shorten your offspring's life. It's hardly surprising that grown-ups found the need to create grotesque creatures and sinister beings that would act as deterrents. Some of these nightmare characters hide far more sinister and twisted messages than we might think.

The Big Bad Wolf is a straightforward enough symbol. He is the incarnation of the predatory male, seeking to seduce and deflower unsuspecting girls. It would seem that this popular scare-mongering animal was introduced into children's cautionary tales by women. It was a heck of a lot safer for the teller if she substituted wolves, dwarves, and beasts for the menfolk. In a rural society dominated by males, it probably wasn't in your best interest to bluntly state that menfolk were the real danger. The threat had to be woven into stories of those scary beasts and monsters.

Studies suggest that most of these tales originated in the creative minds of females. There's a distinctly feminine flavour to many of them. Think of all those young women in perilous situations, having to make crucial choices, tasked with solving riddles or problems. The menfolk could always use weapons or their fists to escape, but girls had to rely on their wits. Think about Rapunzel in her tower, Rumpelstiltskin's captured girl, Sleeping Beauty, Snow White, Belle and the beast, Gretel, Little Red Riding Hood, and a host of others.

Let's take the tale of *Rumpelstiltskin*. This seemingly innocent story has much more vulgar elements than we could imagine. This is a German legend that was already well known when the Brothers Grimm had it published in 1812. Skip the next few paragraphs if you know the popular kids' story.

The popular, kids' version

When a miller boasts that his beautiful daughter can spin straw into gold, the claim captures the interest of the king himself. He locks her up in a room in a tall tower. She is to sit at her spinning wheel and convert the heaps of straw into gold for his majesty. If she transforms every last wisp of straw into the yellow stuff, he will marry her.

As an added incentive, if she fails to do it, she'll lose her pretty head. The poor girl, a victim of her father's idle claim, is doomed.

Just when she's given up all hope, a little gnome-like man appears in the room. He's dressed all in yellow and sporting a red hood. He promises to spin all the gold for her if she will give him her first-born child. The baby, of course, would be a prince or princess. She reluctantly agrees, but, when the little man sees her tears, he adds a get-out clause. If she can guess his name within 3 days, he'll let her keep the baby.

The king is delighted with all the gold and plans are already afoot for the wedding. When the little imp visits her again at the castle, she makes numerous wrong guesses at this name. He skips off, delighted that she's failed. Desperate, but still able to think on her feet, she orders a guard to follow the diminutive devil. The trusty guard is to return and tell the princess-in-waiting where the little fella lives. The next day, in possession of this information, the clever girl sneaks off into the neighbouring woods and finds a small cottage in a dell. She hides behind a tree as the little man emerges from his home. He starts to dance about and sing:

Rumpelstiltskin: Oh, now I'll win this clever game.
Rumpelstiltskin is my name.

When the tiny terror reappears at the castle on the 3rd day, to give her one more chance to guess, the girl is ready for him. She tells him the correct name and

Rumpelstiltskin is furious. He jumps up and down, stamping his feet in rage. After quite a bit of this, he manages to split himself completely in two. End of Rumpelstiltskin and end of story.

The older, dirtier versions

What exactly is this troubling yarn really about? I've found some older, more salacious, versions of Rumpelstiltskin. The midget's name, for one thing, is thought to have meant 'wrinkled foreskin' in a Proto-West Germanic language. The stilt part of the name being a bygone slang term for the male member. The story seems to have been adapted and toned-down for younger listeners over the generations.

In one earlier telling, the manic gnome attempts to leap into the girl's mouth to stop her saying his name. In another rendition, he jumps up and down, pulling at his hood until he explodes. Freud would have a field day with that. The much earlier renderings of the tale seem to have been designed to warn young women against rape, masturbation, unwanted pregnancy, and making hasty promises to men.

Why would she agree to hand over her first-born child? Well, considering that the alternative is beheading, it's clearly the lesser of two evils for the desperate girl. More puzzling though, is why the little chap would want the baby in the first place. Again, this element of the story has been cleaned up for younger ears. The older German narrative sees Rumpelstiltskin demanding that she bear a child for him. This is something very different. Not only does he wish to have his wicked way with this beauty, but he also plans to impregnate her.

Little Red Riding Hood has equally shocking origins. The old French expression for a maiden's loss of her virginity was elle avoit vu le loup – she's seen the wolf. In the original tale, Red is persuaded to join wolfy in grandma's bed. He then gobbles her up, just as he did with her unsuspecting granny. So, agreeing to hop into bed with a wolf/bloke results in a horrible death for the young lass. Again, this sounds like an older woman's warning to a young girl.

As for Snow White? Well, in the darker, earlier narrative, it's Snow White's own mum that sends her the poisoned apple. Her own beauty fading, Mrs White is insanely jealous of her own daughter's good looks. The poor girl eats the deadly fruit and drops dead. Cinderella's got her horrid stepmother and twisted ugly sisters to torment her. Gretel and her little brother are sent out into the dark wood by their stepmom. She's no longer willing to feed them and is desperate to get rid of them. When they stumble upon a gingerbread house, its owner, a cannibalistic witch, plans to have them for supper.

So, in folklore, where there's evil mums, stepmothers, queens, or females of any kind, it's generally jealousy that's driving them to evil deeds. The message is for girls to be on their guard against those women who would resent their youth and beauty. The wolf wants to seduce you and the older dames don't want any younger competition. In short, your youthfulness, good looks, and purity don't last long, so guard them closely.

The appearances of witches in traditional folk stories is an altogether different thing. They seem to be an anomaly. Their inclusion in stories such as Hansel and Gretel and Snow White warns that some women can also be a source of danger for unwary children. Like talking wolves and angry little goblins, witches don't exist. The majority of our ancestors did believe in them though. As far as Mediaeval mums and dads were concerned, there really were spellcasting, child-eating old hags out there in the woods.

Once again it's the woods that the little 'uns should steer clear of. The use of the dark wood as a setting for the various fairy tale horrors should not surprise us. In a past age, not too far back from their own time, a huge percentage of Europe was covered in trees.

By the 17th Century, when many of these tales were first recorded, although much depleted, the forests and great woods still dominated. Most villages and towns were within spitting distance of many trees. This is the reason why virtually all the birds we see in our gardens and parks are woodland birds. We harvested most of the timber, but the woodland creatures remain.

The Pied Piper. Solved!

After years of research into this legend, I reckon I've tracked down the mysterious Pied Piper figure. He was right under our noses all the time. Another surprise is that the rats and children didn't actually follow him from Hamelin. He scared them the Hell outta town. The stuff that I unearthed seems to make a lot more sense than what we've been told before.

Part of the confusion with this story comes from his name, or lack of it, as it turns out. The Pied Piper of the children's story isn't given a name. In all the versions that I've checked, the Mayor of Hamelin and his council never ask for their visitor's name. Heck, they don't even ask him what he's doing there in their rat-infested town. This is because they already know who he is.

To discover exactly who he was, and what he was doing in Hamelin, I had to answer two crucial questions:

What is the identity of The Pied Piper and what else did he do, other than flush out rats?

Exactly what kind of pipe did he play?

O.K. I'm sorry. I know the first one is really two questions, but, seriously, answering them was absolutely crucial if I was ever going to get to the bottom of this sinister fable. Please skip the next two paragraphs if you know the traditional tale. Here it is.

The traditional tale of The Pied Piper

The children's version takes the form of a straightforward moral story. Dressed in a colourful jester-like costume, and playing a jaunty tune on his pipe, the stranger arrives in Hamelin town in Saxony. It's the early 13th Century and the place is over-run with a plague of rats. When the stranger offers to rid the town of the vermin, the mayor and council members readily agree to his terms – a bag of silver coins. Sure enough, that same day, the Pied Piper plays his tune and every rat in Hamelin follows him down to the river Weser and jumps in.

With the rats drowned, the jolly chap returns to the town hall and asks for his reward. The mayor tells him to come back tomorrow as they haven't got the funds ready yet. Keen to be on his way, the musician returns in the morning and knocks on the door of the town hall. There is no answer. He calls at the mayor's house. Nobody answers the door there either. Aware that they have no intention of paying him for ridding them of their problem, he takes up his pipe again and plays. This time, all the children of the town follow him as he heads out to the surrounding countryside. They accompany him to a rocky hillside far from Hamelin. The cliff face opens, and all the children disappear into the darkness. The cliff opening slams shut and they are never seen again.

The man with the owl pipe

It is said that there was, until the late 17th Century, a coloured glass window in a Hamelin church that depicted this story. That church was destroyed by fire though, and all we've got to go on is speculation. There is, however, a 16th century painting of The Pied Piper that's claimed to be copied from that window. What appears to be going on in this early Piper picture is the opposite of what the traditional story tells us.

Before we get a glimpse of the real Pied Piper, let's get the whole children's crusades nonsense out of the way.

Sometime, late in the last century, a feasible explanation suddenly appeared. Two doomed children's crusades, both in the 13th Century were suggested as sources for the story. One of these, in 1212, it was said, saw thousands of children from France and Germany march off to regain the Holy Land from the Muslims. We're told that a French and a German lad both claimed to have had visions of the Virgin Mary. She instructed them to gather a great army of children to win back the sacred Bible places through peaceful means. That would help to explain the town being emptied of children. They didn't happen though.

Historians in the 1970's made it clear that there were some wandering bands of adults that set out for the Middle East with evangelical motives, but definitely no army of children.

If we want to know who The Pied Piper really was, and what he was up to, we need look no further than a merry trickster who was already well known by the early 16th Century. In Germany, the low countries, Denmark, Poland, and Italy, a character called Till Eulenspiegel appeared in many stories. Dressed in a jolly jester-like costume (usually half yellow and half red, and complete with fool's cap), the crafty prankster got up to all sorts of chicanery.

He's even depicted in some places with musical instruments, including a pipe. It's not uncommon to find woodcuts of him surrounded by delighted children. In stories dating from 1500 onwards, he's described as an avenger and a judge of humanity, a cynic who shows people that, for all their airs and graces, they're 'no better than mice or rats.' That's an interesting choice of animals.

So, they're, 'no better than mice or rats'? That line is quoted directly from a 16th century book of traditional German stories called *Waldgeschichten und Bunte Leute*. The particular story I've taken it from is about Till Eulenspiegel. It looks to me like someone, somewhere in the past, has taken Till's metaphoric rats and turned them into real live vermin.

I couldn't find any convincing Pied Piperish stuff that pre-exists good old Till. He's the first figure that fits the profile. There's a couple of references to a 14th century book that some bloke was, 'reported to have owned'. There's no sign of it today though. Other than a single sentence in the 15th century *Lüneburg manuscript*, we've only got a bunch of distinctly dodgy sources to guide us.

In the stories I read, Till's chief aim was to reveal the evil and weakness in others. One of his specialities was to trick folk into eating his faeces. This is not what you'd call high-brow stuff. Many of his japes involved crude behaviour of one kind or another. Eulenspiegel means 'owl mirror'. Eulenspiegel justifies his cruel tricks by claiming that, like a mirror, he's only showing folk their own stupidity, hypocrisy, and follies. What about the owl part of his name? Weirdly, it seems to be linked to the rats idea.

There is another plausible way that rats found their way into the tale. The German word for plague is pest. With this in mind, it's not difficult to see how some non-German speaker has misinterpreted pest as vermin. There's no suggestion that, at that time, rats would be linked to plague. It's simply a misunderstanding. Yes, but what about owls?

Now, with an army of rats added to the story, an alleged church window depiction, the plague in Europe, and the popularity of Till Eulenspiegel, everything is almost in place for the famous tale to emerge. Almost though. We still need to account for the owl part of his name. In German and Belgian folklore, if a priest had a plague of rats in his church (Yes. The word 'plague' was actually used in the source I found) he offered the tower for an owl to live in. Once the owl was in residence, the rats departed en masse.

Another pre-13th Century German saying claims that the hoot of an owl signifies the impending death of a child.

German culture of the period associated owls with witchcraft, casting spells, and killing babies. These beliefs can be dated back to Roman times. The Romans had a strong and lengthy presence in Germany. Here's the clincher though.

The Pied Piper, as the name suggests, plays a pipe. But what manner of pipe was he supposed to have played. Could it have been an owl pipe? Owl pipes have been around for hundreds of years. Examples have been found in Northern Europe, dating back to the 7th century AD. Most have been found in ancient churches, assumed to have been used by a choir master to sound the right note. I reckon that they were there to scare the crap out of rats and mice. If the priest couldn't persuade an owl to move in, impersonating one was the next best thing.

A 15th century pottery and horn owl pipe.

The pipes were made from pottery, wood, or horn. Sometimes, they're a combination of these. Although they have owl images on them, I have no idea what they sound like. It'd be hoot-like notes, I guess. The one I saw has two finger holes in place of the owl's eyes.

It was the call of an owl that signalled the imminent death of children, or scared rats into leaving a church. I'll bet it was the second of these that the pipes were designed for.

It's reasonable to think that these particular instruments were intended to fool rats and mice into thinking there was an owl attack on the way. They only have a few holes in them; that's all you'd need for an owl call. As far as I can see, this is the only way we can explain why the town's vermin would skedaddle when he toots on his pipe.

The very earliest painting of The Pied Piper, from 1592, shows the rats fleeing from the sound of his instrument. It's absolutely clear that they're not following him; they're about half a mile ahead of him, racing up a hill. This painting is said to be a copy of the 13th century church window picture from Hamelin itself. There's also a mid-16th century woodcut that shows the children leaving the town, heading for a hillside, and there's no Pied Piper in sight. Presumably, he's way behind them, out of shot.

The name Eulenspiegel can easily be read as owl impersonator, or perhaps, owl copier. After all, that's what mirroring means. I think this is what the Pied Piper was meant to be doing? He was clearing out the town's rats with the sound of an owl. They weren't following him;

he was driving them out. He uses the same trick on the children.

These folklore warnings could well have been foremost in the mind(s) of whoever dreamed up the Pied Piper story as we know it today. The onset of the plague in a town like Hamelin would have surely made people even more susceptible to the powerful messages of old beliefs. Every owl hoot would seem portentous to worried parents. A stranger in your town might well bring the plague with him. In 1361 there are accounts of the plague devastating the child population. It seems that, in many outbreaks, they were the worst affected.

The Pied Piper was a derivation of Till Eulenspiegel. He wasn't using magic to clear Hamelin of vermin. He was blowing on a device that, although not at all common, actually existed at the time. The story is just another one of Till's tricks, another of his dramatic statements that show other folk the consequences of their foolishness.

"You didn't pay me, so you've brought this on yourselves."

Fairy tales are always about danger. The perils that threatened children in the mediaeval world are not too far removed from those that menace them today. The wolves and other horrors of the nearby forest have been exchanged for on-line child groomers, paedophile priests, and dodgy TV presenters.

It's just people now that we protect our children from. It's always been people though. The wolves, witches, and other scary beings that mediaeval kids were told to keep clear of were actually human beings. The traditional anthropomorphising of various beasts and monsters wasn't just to add colour to the stories. The tellers knew full well that it was certain men who'd prey on their young ones. It was mostly men that young girls were to be wary of.

All the fairy tale baddies are just ways of expressing threats that are closer to home for the kids. We're still doing this sort of thing today.

Whether they are generalisations, like 'the man in the street', or 'the average teenager…', or faceless threats, such as terrorists, they're a way that we have of reducing a mass of individuals into one. I think that it's a method through which we are able to cope better with the sheer diversity of the groups we're talking about. This is really what those storytellers of the past were doing. It's more reasonable to expect that a 7-year-old would retain the idea of one big bad bad-guy rather than a host of them.

Adults told disturbing folk stories to fix the dangers in their children's minds. I'm willing to bet that kids in those days were in every way as dismissive of adult advice as they are today. When I taught for a living, I became increasingly aware of the impact that visiting Theatre in Education (TIE) groups had on our students.

The very same warnings that teachers were straining to get across in PSHE sessions were made more palatable and genuinely memorable by these young professional actors. Our pupils would have enjoyed the plays they presented, regardless of their messages. The characters were young teenage boys and girls, faced with key life choices about sex, using the internet, drugs, alcohol, and exploitative scenarios of all kinds. Like their 17th century and Mediaeval counterparts, they loved a good story involving kids their own ages. They were more receptive because the stories were about dangers that they were already vaguely aware of. Whether they were big bad wolves, or internet perverts, the inclusion of these figures made sense to them. They were clearly identified as the bad guys – the ones to be wary of.

The Wizard of Odd

I've investigated many claims of phantom appearances, but I've only ever had one ghostly experience myself. I mean I've seen and heard something that I can't explain rationally. Thinking about it makes me shiver. I still have to remind myself that it really happened.

It was 1998. I was supply teaching at a lovely secondary school in Leeds. The Drama teacher was putting on a production of 'The Wizard of Oz'. I got roped into helping her get the production together. No sooner than we'd started rehearsals, the Drama teacher was taken ill and signed off for months. Before I could stop myself, I'd volunteered to direct the show. As you can imagine, there was a huge cast. One 12-year-old pupil had landed the role of a Munchkin and asked if her dog could be in the cast? She was genuinely excited at the prospect. I told her that we already had a parent's mutt available for the role of Dorothy's doggy. She pointed to the empty floor to her right and informed me that her pet dog was right here, and she was a 2-year-old red setter, called Molly. She'd take any role I'd like to give her.

I was relieved that I wouldn't have to turn her down. Beaming, I told her that Molly could have a role as a Munchkin dog and so stay close to her on stage. The girl frowned for a moment and revealed that Molly was much too big for a Munchkin pet. I was just about to offer an alternative part when she suddenly smiled and explained that she would shrink Molly to the right size for a Munchkin. Problem solved!

The rehearsals went well, and the cast had grown comfortable with the invisible canine member of their company. One afternoon though I jokingly mentioned to the boys and girls that I hoped Molly wouldn't disgrace herself on our lovely stage. Well, that was a huge mistake.

Molly's owner was outraged. She informed me, in no small measure, that Molly was a well-trained pet and had never done anything so horrible. This was followed by a storming off stage and a dumb silence from the rest of us. She hadn't taken umbrage for long though. Girl and dog were back for the next week's rehearsal and, after I'd apologised and agreed to put Molly's name in the programme, we were on good terms again.

The first couple of rehearsals went well. It wasn't until we brought Butch, the real live dog, on stage that the weirdness started. He was the three-year-old Labrador playing the role of Toto. Suddenly, we had, in theory, two dogs in the scene.

Sitting out front, script in hand, I called for the Munchkins to enter from stage right. This was to be the first time these loveable little creatures appeared on stage. Dorothy and Toto were alone in Munchkin land at that moment.

The adorable little Years 7 and 8 Munchkin chorus came onto stage. Molly was among them. The other kids had given our invisible cast member all the space she needed.

All Hell broke loose. Butch, savagely barking and foaming at the muzzle, broke free from Dorothy. The otherwise docile Labrador shot across the stage, scattering terrified Munchkins in all directions. Most of them ran off into the wings or hid behind flats. Molly's owner, eyes wide with panic, hurriedly scooped up her tiny invisible pooch and legged it for the wing.

I only just managed to get to Butch, just as he was about to leap up at the retreating girl. Jumping onto the stage, I slipped my hand under his collar and wrestled him to the deck. I lay there, badly winded and with the shrill screams of a dozen Munchkins bursting my eardrums.

Teaching Assistants were soon on hand to help restore calm in the hall. Butch was sent home in disgrace, bundled into his (parent) owner's car. I was recovering with a cup of coffee whilst Molly's keeper was speaking soothing words to her spectral pet. What the heck had just happened?

As you can imagine, within minutes, the rabid dog scene was the talk of the school. I was called before The Head Teacher and asked to explain things. I couldn't. It was inexplicable.

The production continued without Butch. Doug Farmer from the Technology department constructed an amazing radio-controlled Toto. He operated the little Yorkshire Terrier robot from the wing. Doug was an engineering genius. All went well until a main character dropped out.

Kieran, the boy who played The Cowardly Lion had allergies. These included very bad reactions to dog and cat fur. As soon as we'd started rehearsing his first scene, his eyes swelled up. Even though there were no Munchkins on stage, they were still there, backstage with the spectral dog. He sneezed, coughed and, even though he tried, he couldn't speak or sing. I couldn't quite take all this in. Were they just taking the piss out of me?

Well, no. Of course, they weren't doing that. Everyone wanted the musical to be a big success. It just seemed that, despite its incorporeality, there WAS a dog on stage. Like all the children in the show, I was always patient and understanding with Molly's owner. The closest I came to losing it with her was when she asked if she could have a word with me about Toto. She complained that the remotely controlled dog was, 'freaking Molly out'. Was it possible, she wondered, if we could cut the robo-dog from the production and let Dorothy just mime a dog on a lead?

I was almost speechless. I don't know if it was my frustration, anger, or the irony of the situation that took my breath away. Here she was suggesting that both dogs should be invisible. After all, her Munchkin mutt was a kindly concession on my part. Everyone else was delighted with Doug's dog-bot. Toto was a big hit with the cast. I managed to say no. She just shrugged in response. I was secretly hoping that she would be the next to drop out of the show.

By this stage everyone was aware of the strange goings-on with Molly. We had a new, allergy-free Cowardly Lion and the curtain was about to go up for the first night. Surprisingly, apart from one issue, it went off very well.

Few lines were dropped, the lights and sound worked superbly, and the actors did us all proud. It was the 'one issue' that added to the puzzle.

The Stage Manager, Mrs Smith, told me at the interval that, backstage, the crew could hear odd animal sounds in their earphones. She had checked with the Front-of-house people and, sure enough, there were doggy-like panting and whining sounds coming through the P.A. system. It was only happening now and then and, as far as the audience were concerned, was meant to be part of the show.

After all, Toto was a dog and dogs make noises.

I checked with Doug. No. He assured me that robotic Toto had no sound effects functions. I asked all the kids with mics if anyone was making those sounds near them. Again, no. There was only one other possibility and I refused to give it credibility.

The whole run was a success. Everyone involved was on a high after the last night. As was the custom, all the cast and crew signed a card for yours truly, the director. Molly's owner had even added a paw print. It looked incredibly realistic. I almost asked her how she'd made it look so good. That'd be a foolish question though. As far as she was aware, Molly was as real as you or I.

It's twenty-three years later. I still can't quite wrap my head around the whole ghostly dog idea. I'm meant to solve this sort of thing. The problem is, I can't find a really solid explanation; the sort of answer that ticks all the rational boxes.

Was it all a big wind-up by the cast and crew after all? No, it wasn't that. The massive hoax idea was my last hope for a genuine, solid explanation and there was too much to disprove it. The Cowardly Lion's dog allergy was confirmed by his parents. He had a week off school after his attack. Butch's owner said that he only chased and barked at other dogs, never people.

Also, it's very unlikely that the Stage Manager and Sound Crew would sabotage their own production. There was simply too much at stake for anyone to make that kind of mischief. So...case unsolved.

There was one other case involving an 'imaginary' character. It happened about a year after the whole phantom doggy thing. She was a human child; the supposed invention of a four-year-old girl. This one is another head-scratcher. Even after all these years, I can't find an explanation for Georgina.

A close friend's 4-year-old girl, Sophie, talked to them about Georgina Green, a girl that she'd met at her reception class in school. Sophie's folks had every reason to believe that Georgina was just that – a school pal. Sophie told them where Georgie (her pet-name) lived and all about her younger brother, Charlie. It all made perfect sense. After a few days, Sophie's mum was keen to arrange an after-school play date for the two girls. It was only when Sophie informed them that Georgie had her own collection of living, breathing, prehistoric dinosaurs, that they got suspicious.

Sophie's parents, Ken and Gwen Clarke, discovered that her teacher had not heard of a girl called Georgina Green in the school. The worried parents told the teacher about Sophie's detailed accounts of her friend's personality, family, and likes. Teacher reassured them that their daughter's invented friend only confirmed what she already had suspected – that Sophie has a wonderfully fertile imagination.

The stories she had written in class, and her drawings backed this up. Gwen and Ken learned that Sophie hadn't, at that point, made friends with anyone in her class. Sophie did make real friends as the term went on. When her parents asked her about Georgie, they were told, without a trace of sadness, that she'd moved schools. Plausible right up to the end.

Or is that the end? I'm not so sure about that. My wife, Lizzy, and I were babysitting one evening, about a year after her imaginary pal had gone. I asked Sophie which school Georgina had moved to? She hesitated for a second. It wasn't a pause to invent a school though. She was clearly remembering its name.

"St Mary's", she replied with confidence.

St Mary's was about seven miles away, on the outskirts of Bradford. I asked if she still kept in touch with her.

"Not really. I see her sometimes when I'm out shopping with Mum and Dad. We say hi then."

That should have put an end to the whole shebang, shouldn't it? Well, no. Not at all. It's what she told me next that really got my interest.

"She (Georgina) is in the same school as Penny."

That was intriguing. Penny is my friend Peter's daughter. Like Sophie, she was five at this time and, as we'd told Sophie, was attending St Mary's. Sophie had met Penny when she and her dad had visited me and Lizzy.

Ken and Gwen had dropped by that day with Sophie. It was a briefish meeting. Sophie and her parents were just leaving for home as Peter and Penny arrived. They couldn't have exchanged more than a few words. I needed to check with Peter. I rang Peter the next day. He passed the 'phone to Penny. Sure enough, Penny confirmed that there was a girl in her class called Georgina Green. She'd started at an early stage of her first year. I asked her to describe Georgina. Her description exactly matched that of Sophie's.

When I explained the whole thing to her dad, Peter was also puzzled. He was as adamant as I that they hadn't discussed the imaginary girl at their one and only meeting. He promised that he'd check up with Penny's teacher and get back to me tomorrow.

Up until Peter rang me the next evening, I had abandoned completely all rational thoughts on this matter. It was Lizzy's occasional sigh and raised eyebrows that told me all I needed to know about her stance on this issue. The 'phone rang at seven.

Peter told me that Penny's teacher knew of no pupil called Georgina Green in the school. She did, however, tell him that she was glad he'd rang because she was a little concerned about Penny's lack of friends. It seemed that she'd moved class at the start of that term and, like Sophie a year before, hadn't really forged any bonds yet. I could have left it there. I couldn't though. I met up with Peter in Leeds at the weekend. He had spoken to Penny about her classmate.

Peter and his wife, Shona, had often heard Penny chatting to herself. They'd both assumed that, having no siblings yet, she had made some imaginary friends. They had asked her about Georgina. No, she told them, Georgina had never been in their house. She was just another kid in her class and not really a friend. She told them that when they heard her chatting, she was talking to her toys.

Surely Sophie had told Penny all about Georgina? That had to be it! Well, both girls fervently denied that. According to Sophie, she'd never mentioned Georgina Green to Penny. Both girls were clearly being 100% truthful in those denials. That's the sort of kids they were.

Lizzy persuaded me to let the matter drop. She'd often had cause to listen patiently to me wittering on about bizarre stuff that nobody else seemed to bother about. I couldn't help wondering about it though.

Was it just a coincidence? I mean, why not? Both girls could have dreamed up the same name for an invisible classmate. It'd be a strange world if there were no coincidences. I mean, in this case, is it any weirder than the other explanations?

Alternatively, Georgina Green might have been the name of a character they'd both read about or watched on TV. I've never checked up on that. If you're reading this and you know of such a fictional character, popular around the turn of the century, you've solved this.

The girls are in their early twenties now. Sophie's studying Psychology at one of our thousands of universities. Penny is a manager at Tesco's. Neither of them remembers Georgina at all. I wonder if Georgina remembers Sophie and Penny?

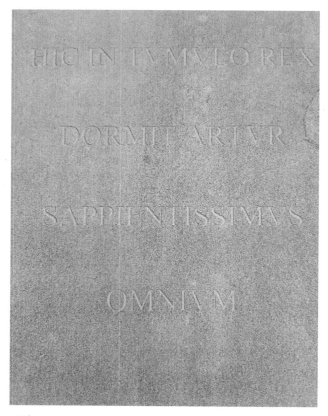

The engraved writing on King Arthur's
memorial stone.

THE REAL KING ARTHUR.

Twice now, I've stumbled upon a real gold nugget, a bit of evidence that shines a bright light into one of those shadowy legends. This one took my breath away. Imagine finding something so unique, so sought after, that it would turn an ancient myth into fact?

Thirty-four years ago I had a job at The University of Leeds. I was employed in the main office, but, on one occasion, my boss, asked me to help out in their Archives room. We were clearing out very old copies of post grad. Theses. These works were from way back. Some were written by people who are famous today, like J.R.R. Tolkien, for instance. It wasn't the faded, purple lettered carbon copy of his MA piece that stood out for me though. It was something altogether more surprising, shocking perhaps.

The pair of us were to take the works to another department to be scanned into a computer. That isn't to say we didn't read bits and pieces from one or two of them before we bagged them up. One piece, and one name in particular, left me speechless.

It was a section from a paper titled, *Late Roman Britain: The politics of the power shift.* It was written in the early 1930s by a student who, I later discovered, became curator of a well-known museum in London. Amongst a fascinating section on the struggles to fill the power vacuum left by The Roman's, there was mention of 'Artur' of the Dumnonii tribe'. There was a translated section of an early 9th century text, *Rex Lamentatio*. It described the heroics of Celtic warriors in their 5th century struggles against invading Saxons.

Written around 820 AD, the extract was mostly just a list of names, but there were a couple of brief descriptions of events. Here's the (translated) bit about Artur:

At this time (494 AD) at Nonstallon there came a host (Presumably Saxons) against Cornwall's King Mark. At the riverside, there fought bravely, Artur and Cai with 800 men and overcame a greater number of the host. 2000 of the enemy were slain and the river (River Camel?) ran red for a week. Banners, swords, and shields were taken by the king and his warriors.

The bracketed comments are mine. I'm pretty sure that Nonstallon is a spelling variation of Nanstallon in Cornwall. The river's name 'Camel' hints at Camelot, Arthur's legendary castle. It seemed likely to me that the warrior 'Artur' mentioned here is the legendary Arthur. In this case, he's serving Cornwall's King Mark.

My belief was strengthened by the mention of 'Cai' who fought alongside him.

Surely here was the Sir Kay (in English) who sat at Arthur's Round Table of knights? The same Cai that appears in the ancient Welsh *Mabinogion* tale of Culwych and Olwyn. Records put his birth around 468 AD. That'd fit in neatly with the 494 AD date for the battle, making him twenty-six at the time.

The 13th century French Vulgate Cycle mentions the Holy Grail quest beginning in the late 5th century, so, again, the timing matched. I'd stumbled upon a 9th century record of King Arthur. The most thrilling thing was the fact that this was, as far as I know, the only one that (almost) accurately spells his name.

Previous written mentions of 'Artorius' or 'Artorus' seem to be references to the Roman General Lucius Artorius Castus who lived in the 2nd century AD. There's no connection between him and the heroic Arthur of the romances. Here though, I had in my hand the first historic record of the figure we recognise today as Arthur.

In those pre-smartphone days, making a written copy of the section, or a quick photocopy of the page were the only options open to me.

The notes at the back of his thesis told me that the only known copy of *Rex Lamentatio*, was in the library of Holland House. This place, Lord Ilchester's 17th century home, had an extensive collection of old texts. The next day was Saturday so, I was off to our capital city to try and get a look at the book.

I could have saved myself a journey by making a 'phone call. I was impetuous though and booked my train. Holland House, it appears, was badly burned in 1940, during an air raid. And, yes, you've no doubt guessed, the library's book collection was destroyed. I was told by one of the staff though that, in the pre-blitz days, the library was open to the public, by appointment only. Well, that was something at least. Did they still have any records of who'd made appointments, I wondered? Amazingly, they did. They'd been kept in the curator's office and had survived the bomb. Could I have a peek at them? I could! Excellent.

Bingo! Our thesis writer's name was there. On Tuesday 16th February 1932 he'd signed in at 10 am and signed out at 2 pm. I suppose they must have let him take sandwiches in for lunch. So, he had seen the text 'in the flesh' so to speak.

I had booked into a little hotel in Acton for one night, so that have me just one more day in London to get any kind of lead. I needed a clue, something that'd give me a break in my Arthurian case. The next morning, my persistence paid off. It was at The British Library, that firm favourite with pre-internet scholars, that my confidence got a massive boost. That boost came hard in the heels of crushing disappointment though.

I asked one of the librarians if they had any information about *Rex Lamentatio*. After a search through records, the kind lady revealed that, although they hadn't a copy there, they'd briefly had a one on loan in 1921. Would I like to know where that copy was now?

My exhilaration lasted about a second, before it dawned on me that she was referring to the incinerated Holland House copy. However, all was not lost. It appeared that, about a year ago, an Exeter University student had also made the same enquiry as me. She remembered it because that was the first time she'd heard of the text. Someone was clearly working the same case. I needed to find that person.

Like myself, he'd signed in at the library, so finding his name was a cinch. I pledged infinite gratitude if she would find me his name, and, to my utter delight, she did. He was Mark Hick. I just hoped that Exeter would be as helpful as my library angel.

After a brief return to the library, to give my saviour a box of Terry's All Gold chocolates, I found a phone box and got through to The Post Graduate office at Exeter.

I got through to a terribly officious sounding chap who, initially, gave me short shrift. On no account would they give out a student's contact details, be they past or current. When I explained that we seemed to be working on the same idea for our theses, and I wished to share information, he seemed to soften a little. He agreed to 'phone the student and if he got the OK, would pass on his number to me. I waited while he did just that.

A few minutes later I was talking to a student called Mark Hick.

Mark was thirty-six, and a post-graduate. He lived in Truro though.

As a self-confessed folklore fanatic, he was just as excited as I was about finding someone else who'd heard of the mysterious, *Rex Lamentatio*. His PhD thesis was focused on England's early post-Roman era and he had a particular interest in King Arthur. He insisted that I stay with him for a few days in Truro. I thanked him heartily, hung up, and headed for Paddington Station.

Mark, a tall, thin chap with a bushy red beard, met me at the station. After he'd installed me in his spare room, we popped down to his local, The Globe, for beers, fish and chips, and a planning session.

The next morning, he'd drive us up to the coast, to Perranporth. There, he assured me, was strong evidence of King Arthur's last resting place. Like me, it seemed, his search for Arthur hadn't been side-tracked by the dozens of dodgy locations identified as Arthurian landmarks. We'd both discarded all the tourist luring tosh. He was interested in actual evidence, the stuff you see and touch. Tomorrow, he'd show me one such piece.

This was thrilling. Meeting a fellow enthusiast, fish and chips, Cornish beer...and now this! It was hard to see how life could get any better. Well, the next morning, it did. We were up at 6am. Mark shoved an enormous rubber torch, a roll of gaffer tape, two snorkel masks, scissors, and two pairs of overalls into a duffel bag. He grabbed two towels from a cupboard and crammed them in as well.

"You should bring a change of clothes, Phil. I've got another set in the car. We're going to get a proper soaking."

I popped a pair of corduroys, a tee-shirt, socks, boxers, and a thick jersey into my rucksack. Snorkels? What the heck did we need those for?

Just to the north of Perranporth in West Cornwall are a series of old, abandoned tunnels. They are the remnants of an ancient tin mine. The Cornish folk had mined treasured ores, concealed beneath their land, for hundreds of years.

After a short drive North, to the coast, Mark parked up at Droskyn Point. We followed a narrow, rocky track, heading South from the beach towards the sheer, black cliff. The raised path spiralled down towards the tall, jagged rock face. Sea water slopped at either side of our slightly elevated route. It led to a narrow sea inlet that extended far into the rock.

The flooded mine. This is the place where we found the stone. Albert Russ/Shutterstock.com

Here, he told me, was one entrance to a labyrinthine network of millennia old mining tunnels. Mark and his pals used to come here as boys, to play adventure games. There were scores of passages, but some are now underwater. It was one of these submerged shafts that we were going to inspect. Well, that explained the swimwear and snorkels. We stopped in the shadowy entrance, and

Mark emptied the contents of the bag onto the sandy ground.

We put the overalls on, and Mark applied rings of gaffer tape around the ankle, wrists, and neck holes. It's not completely waterproof, he confessed, but it would do. Snatching the rubber torch, he led us into the vast darkness of the mines.

Despite the yellow cone of the torch, the blackness surrounding us was overwhelming. Breathing was more difficult. We trudged on, turning right, then left. Left again. Now we seemed to be descending gradually. Mark warned me that there would be debris of varying sizes to negotiate.

"Oh, and it's going to be quite cold down there", he added. There's about two feet headroom above the water's surface, so try not to bash your head when we surface."

I told him that I wasn't a particularly good swimmer.

Mark reassured me that no swimming was required. We'd be walking cautiously through a long tunnel with our snorkels peeking out above the surface. His torch was 100% waterproof, so we could see clearly.

I had, naively, pictured a gentle, gradual descent, like walking from the shallow to the deep ends of a swimming pool. This was nothing like that. Mark shone the beam into a narrow, shoulders width, hole to our immediate right. I could just make out the water's surface a couple of feet into the opening.

We put the snorkel masks on. Mark lowered himself down into the gap. As I followed, it struck me that this was a side tunnel whose entrance had partially collapsed. I was now up to my chin in icy black water. Mark was right about the overalls. They weren't completely waterproof. I'd never been so cold in my life. And that's coming from someone who's visited Ebbw Vale in January.

This was scary. The eerie torchlight gave us plenty of visibility though. Mark turned and made a gesture that we should submerge and, heads bent, down we went. We'd disturbed a small cloud of sandy particles, but, otherwise, the water was crystal clear. My body was slowly adjusting to the cold. This was amazing. It was like a dream.

There were bits of what looked like stone blocks here and there; they were definitely hand-worked, shaped into oblongs. What the heck were they doing down here? A couple of little crabs scuttled about.

Mark turned and drew my attention to a larger block of stone ahead of us, lying against the tunnel wall. As we approached it, I could see it was a memorial stone of some kind, lying on its side. It was approximately 50 cm high and 35 cm wide. Made from granite, I'd say. A small stone, but, as it turned out, an incredibly heavy one. There was an inscription.

Holding our breaths we ducked down to get a closer look at the writing. What I read there was astounding. In shallowly carved capital letters:

HIC IN TVMVLO REX DORMIT ARTVR

SAPPIENTISSIMVS OMNIVM

HERE, IN THIS TOMB, SLEEPS KING ARTUR

WISEST OF ALL MEN

Wow! Now I could fully grasp Mark's excitement about this trip. I had a thousand questions, but they'd have to wait until we'd surfaced. Mark mimed that we should continue our sub aqua journey, further down the passage. I tore my eyes away from the slab and followed him.

There were more mysterious bits of stone to negotiate. Then, without warning, another opening to our left. This one was wider and framed by more, well worked, narrow stone slabs. There were more capital letters chiselled into them, but no time to linger. Mark trudged on, through the gap, and I followed. I noticed that directly in front of the entrance, the ground rose abruptly by about 10 cm. to form a sort of hard oblong doorstep.

We passed into what looked like a storeroom. It was a water-carved cave, about five metres by ten. There was roughly three metres above the water line here. Below the surface, the sandy floor was littered with smooth pebbles. At the far end, there was a rectangular alcove, the shape of a narrow door, and rising from the floor. Mark pointed

upwards and we surfaced. I was bursting with curiosity.

"This is unbelievable. What is this place? Has the Artur slab been dated yet? What's that alcove thing?"

Mark was grinning. This was probably the first time, since his discovery, that he'd shared the sheer wonder of it all with another human being. He was bubbling over with enthusiasm. He'd discovered the slab months ago but was reluctant to enlist help to bring it out of the caves. It seemed he was anxious to tell as few people as possible about his discoveries. Also, he was pretty certain he couldn't shift the thing on his own. Even the two of us would struggle to lug it out of the tunnel.

As for the small door shaped recess, he hadn't a clue what it was. He'd translated the inscriptions at the entrance though:

iiqiis/custos/mec divinos

Each word was carved on one of the three stone slabs. 'Knight, Guardian, Wizard'. The first word, 'iiqiis was an easier (or lazier) way of carving 'eques', the ii being a quick representation of 'e', and its position in the order of letters suggesting a 'u' before it.

It was incredible to imagine that I was, most possibly, one of only two people who'd read these words in the last 1600 years. A thought occurred to me. Were these three words defining one person or three separate individuals?

Why hadn't the world heard of this incredible discovery?

Well, in the 1980s news travelled a heck of a lot slower than in our computer, internet, Facebook, 21st century.

Unless Mark let it loose on the media, Artur's burial place could remain a mystery indefinitely.

Although they would still need to be dated, Mark was quite confident that these stones were from the 5th century AD. There were, after all, at this time, only two sources for this particular spelling of the king's name: *Rex Lamentatio,* and these amazing slabs of granite.

So, Arthur was a warrior of the Cornish Dumnonii tribe, previously in the service of King Mark, and at this later stage, a king himself. He'd fought successfully against the Saxons, and, presumably, succeeded Mark as ruler. The surviving engravings draw attention to his wisdom as well as his bravery as a leader. This sounded a lot like the fabled king of countless tales. The mention of a wizard was tantalising though. Did this refer to Artur himself, or, dare we imagine, a Merlin figure?

I was so giddy with all this new stuff whirling around in my head that I hadn't noticed my teeth chattering. I was suddenly aware of how bloody cold I felt. Freezing water had seeped in everywhere. Mark was shaking. His overalls were obviously as leaky as mine.

"We'd better get out of here", he said. I've got an idea how we can get the stone up top, but I'll tell you about it when we're warmer...and dried off".

We were famished by the time we got back to Truro. A huge lunch and a few pints settled us nicely. The Globe was packed, but we'd bagged a table and, by now, Mark was in full flow. He was drawing on a napkin with a ballpoint pen.

"You see, I've made this sort of shallow cart. It's a converted sack trolley, but I've built up the sides with wood. There are chains attached here and here to haul it. I've tried it out with some heavy stuff, and I reckon it would carry the granite slab. I've also made this portable winch system, so we could pull it up the slope."

I complimented him on a brilliant bit of engineering, but I couldn't help wondering how many people it would actually take to get it up to beach level?

Mark was suddenly quiet. He took another sip of his beer while seemingly weighing something up

"I've decided to try and recruit a couple of people from my course at Uni. I think we could bring it up with four of us."

I was pleased that he'd already included me in his big recovery plan. I told him that I'd have to get back to Leeds on Sunday, but I'd be available any weekend after that. He explained that he wanted to do the job during the Summer holidays that started in two weeks. I was pretty sure I could get some time off to suit him, but, if not, I'd pack the job in and come to Cornwall anyway.

Mark was going to tell his tutor about his find and ask her advice about getting it properly dated. I said I thought that would be an excellent idea. Mark seemed hugely relieved that he'd run his ideas by me and got a positive response.

So, on Sunday, I was back in Leeds. Mark was busy organising a crew to raise the memorial stone, and I was finding it impossible to concentrate on my job. He

119

promised to 'phone me to keep me up to date with his progress. In the meantime, I'd happened upon a very promising lead. The man whose thesis I'd found, it seemed, was alive and living in Milton Keynes.

Tracking him down turned out to be a piece of cake. One 'phone call did the trick. The London museum that he'd curated were more than happy to pass on his retirement address. So, within a few hours, I'd got his telephone number from a copy of the Milton Keynes directory in Leeds Library.

Over the 'phone, he seemed delighted that I'd followed up on his work. He readily agreed for me to pay him a visit in MK. I fully intended telling him about the memorial stone Mark had found, but not the location. That would remain a secret.

Now, it must be obvious that I've avoided mentioning his name. It's not because he forbade it. It isn't even because my publishers are twitchy about being sued by his estate. It's simply this. Back in the 1930s, when he'd visited Holland House, he hadn't simply made some notes about what he'd read in the *Rex Lamentatio*. He had done a Mr Bean, and removed the page that contained the Artur reference.

He told me this over cups of tea and custard creams in his beautiful home overlooking Willen Lake. Elderly now, and a widower, he confessed that, in a moment of uncontrollable academic zeal, he had slipped a ruler into the book and tore out the page. He was consumed with guilt for ages.

About eight years later, though, when fire had destroyed the book, he realised that he had the only remaining trace of the work. He half joked that he wished he'd stolen the entire book. At least it would have survived.

He could see I was bursting to ask the big question: Did he still have the page? He nodded and smiled gently. Without a word, he eased himself from his soft leather armchair and headed to one of the bookcases that lined one wall. Removing an A4 sized book, he flipped it open and retrieved a faded, beige sheet. He came over and handed it to me.

It was sheepskin, he said. The curly, Tolkienesque, writing was in a brown ink and incredibly neat. It felt smoother to the touch than I'd imagined. The names Artur and Cai could be made out clearly. I spotted a small square of page missing from the top right-hand corner. I must have looked a little puzzled by this.

"This is the real thing", he said. I had a sample of the sheepskin dated, years after I'd swiped it. It was established as late eighth or early 9th century. That would make it the earliest historical reference to Arthur."

Defacing ancient documents seemed to be a bit of a habit with my host.

I was half joking when I asked if I could get a copy of it to show Mark. Imagine my surprise (and delight) when he said I could actually have the original, on a long-term loan. There were two provisos though:

1. On no account could I tell anyone that he'd given it to me.

2. I would have to persuade Mark to let him come along on the recovery mission.

I was so chuffed that I agreed straight away to both conditions. If I'd stopped for a second to consider the possible consequences of taking a seventy-eight-year-old bloke along, I might have hesitated a bit. We celebrated our upcoming adventure with a couple of sherries and Bakewell Tarts.

Whizz forward four weeks, and there we were, back at Perranporth, unpacking Mark's car. There was Mark, his tutor - Clare, me, the elderly book-defacer, and a big unit of a bloke called Euan. Euan, another post grad from Mark's course, lifted the kit-bashed sack trolley from the hatchback like it was a kid's toy. We stood in a circle around Mark's handiwork.

It looked very much like his pencil sketch, solidly built, with a series of chains to drag it with. And there was the ingenious pulley gadget. We were better prepared this time. As well as the snorkel sets, we wore wetsuits borrowed from Exeter Uni's Humanities faculty. Each of us had a builder's helmet with a torch strapped to it. And, just as crucially, it was 5.45am. The sun had barely risen, so it was unlikely that we'd be disturbed.

Mark had been unenthusiastic when I broke the news about our septuagenarian companion. Like me, it was the chance to get our hands on the pilfered page that swung it with him. Clare and Euan were drooling at the chance to get a look at the memorial stone. Grandpa was champing at the bit.

The five of us were staying at Mark's. It was sort of like indoor camping, sleeping bags and bed rolls all over the place. We'd been going over the retrieval plan most of the night, firstly at the pub then with coffees around Mark's dining table. We hadn't had much shuteye, but, amazingly, it was the older guy who looked the liveliest.

Mark led the way. Euan and I brought up the rear, dragging the trolley and singing, 'Heigh-ho, heigh-ho'. The broad plan was to take the slab straight to the university. Clare had a set of keys and she'd arranged with the porter to have the security alarm switched off for a while. We'd photograph it there and, on the following day, Clare and one of her fellow faculty pals would get to work on authenticating it.

So, down we went. Our passage through the watery ways of the mine was, well, uneventful. The trolley was surprisingly easy to tow, but to be honest, Euan took 90% of the strain.

Euan, Clare, and the ex-curator were totally bedazzled by their first look at the memorial stone. After several minutes of awe-inspired gawping, Mark motioned for us to move on.

The water-carved cave was next. Clare and the curator seemed particularly interested in the mysterious alcove-door thing. After much prodding, poking, and measuring, the curator indicated that we should surface for a pow wow. As soon as our heads popped up, Clare turned to Mark.

"Have you got accurate measurements for the memorial stone?"

That was when the penny dropped for the rest of us. The curator and Clare had simultaneously reached the same conclusion. The memorial stone, it appeared, would fit very neatly into this alcovey hole. The thrilling consequence was instantly understood by all of us. We had found King Arthur's final resting place. Where the heck was the opening though?

Suddenly, it was my turn to have a blinding flash of inspiration. I practically blurted it out.

"We're standing in it! This place IS the tomb. We didn't figure that out because there's no door to this room. But...there is a door! We've just walked over it."

For the second time in just a few minutes, the dawning light of awareness shone on us. The curious doorstep at the entrance, that we'd walked over, was a door. Somehow, long ago, it had fallen, or been pulled over. That, of course would explain how the memorial stone had been taken from here. Why it had been abandoned in the mine tunnel is anybody's guess.

It was time to submerge again. We split up to comb every centimetre of the floor for more clues. Mark and I cleared the sand and dirt from the doorstep. It looked like shaped granite, smoother than the memorial stone. There were no inscriptions, but this was the inside surface of the door. If there was writing, it'd be on the underside. There was no way we'd budge it an inch though.

Without warning, Euan was next to us, frantically gesticulating. He'd found something. We followed him back to the alcove. Clare and the curator were on their knees scraping away at the sandy floor beneath it. They'd disturbed so much detritus that visibility was poor. Carefully, they cleared away pebbles and silt that had collected there to reveal something thrilling.

Directly below the alcove, about a meter apart, were a pair of stone U shaped devices, like row locks. They were lying against the wall now, but each had clearly become detached from it. Two small, square holes in the rock face showed how they'd slotted snugly into place.

Their purpose seemed obvious to Clare. Back above the surface, she explained that she'd seen these devices before, at Iron Age burial sites. One of them supported the hilt, and the other the blade of a sword. Excalibur? It was tempting to jump to that conclusion, but, somewhere, in the back of my mind, I seemed to recall that the older texts made no mention of the blade. That legendary sword was a later invention. It was safe to assume that King Arthur/Artur had a blade of some kind, but, if it had hung here, someone had swiped it a long time ago. I can't say I blame them. Good swords have always been eye-wateringly expensive.

By this time, our already over excited group were foaming at the mouths. We agreed to take the sword holders as well as the memorial stone up top. It was Euan who voiced the question that had popped onto my head also:

"Someone must've already moved the stone from here."

How long ago, or who they were would remain a mystery. Also, here, in this sepulchre, there was no trace of a body. If the king had been laid out in a sarcophagus, you might expect to find it there. Still, a lot could've happened in the last fifteen hundred years, or so. It was highly unlikely that we were the only tomb desecrators who'd tried their luck down this mine.

The journey back was tougher than we'd bargained for. We had seriously underestimated two things: the weight of the memorial stone and the fitness of our septuagenarian companion.

Satisfied that there was nothing else to find in the room, Mark put the sword holders into his bag, and we headed for the memorial stone.

It was just as the five of us were man handling the stone onto Mark's trolley combo, that the curator collapsed. I had suspected that something was up before we'd even left the sepulchre. He was beginning to look distinctly dodgy, his hands shaking and a little unsteady on his feet. At the time, I assumed it was because it was flippin' cold down there and, as I've learned since, we older blokes feel the chill more.

What followed was a brief moment of panic and indecision, followed by the only solution possible. Four of us strapped the stone firmly in place on our sub-aqua cart while Mark removed his snorkel set and held him in an upright position with his lolling head above the water. This was made increasingly difficult by the curator's shaking.

The journey up was problematic, not to say completely knackering. At least our patient was still conscious. Mark and Euan opted to take it in turns to give him piggyback rides whilst the other three of us lugged the enormously heavy stone.

The over-complicated looking pulley device turned out to be invaluable. This meant that, when we reached the steeper gradients nearer the entrance, we could winch the trolley up and, finally, out into the open air.

By the time we'd reached the car, he was a bit steadier and more responsive. To our great relief, it seemed he was diabetic and not having a massive stroke, or heart problems as we feared. I fed him Kendal Mint Cake while Clare got him comfortable in the passenger seat. It was only after the long, gruelling task of lifting the slab into the car that Mark saw another problem. The stone was now on the folded down rear seats. It weighed about the same as an African elephant. Thanks to all the bags and gear shoved in the back with it, we couldn't all fit in and still expect the poor old Volvo to actually move.

After a brief period of head scratching and half-baked solutions, we agreed that Clare would drive with the curator as passenger. She did have the University keys after all. Euan, Mark, and I would make our own way by public transport and we'd join up at the university. We would need the trolley later, so it was crammed in, on top of the memorial stone.

I know it's not strictly in the spirit of storytelling, but I am going to cut a long story short here. Many tedious hours later, we met up at the University. It was dark by the time we joined the other two. The aged curator seemed much more coherent and a lot less wobbly. Clare had bagged a room in the basement, a largely empty storage space, thankfully, serviced by a lift.

The final leg of the Artur stone's trip was a short one, from car, through a back entrance, to the service lift, then down to the basement room. At last, with a combination of excitement and exhaustion, we laid it flat on the floor and stood around admiring our prize.

Photographs were taken, measurements made, and theories exchanged. The curator was struck by how similar the writing was to a stone that had been dug from a 5th century hill fort. Clare recognised similarities with the mid-5th century Latinus Stone from Scotland.

The pair of them flipped through textbooks, humming and hahing over pictures of similar finds. Mark, Euan, and I seemed to be superfluous to needs, so we popped out for a few beers. Mark recommended The Ship Inn, a lovely old boozer that served good food. The agreement was that Clare, and the old tomb robber would lock up and join us when they were ready.

The superb beer, Cornish Pastys and crisps upped our energy levels. We were in good company at The Ship Inn; Francis Drake used to wet his whistle there when he wasn't scouring the seas for enemy ships. Like us, he wasn't averse to the odd bit of tomb raiding from time to time.

It was there, bathing in the warming comfort of the food and beer, that Mark raised an important question.

"Who did the memorial stone actually belong to?"

Until that moment, it hadn't occurred to us that someone probably had ownership. Was it Exeter University? Was it the local council where we found it? Was it treasure trove and therefore property of The Government? Euan was content to let Clare sort that out. Mark was less happy about that option. After all, he'd found the thing and, before he'd done so, nobody had a clue it was down there. When the other two joined us, we had an answer of sorts.

Clare reckoned that it should remain at Exeter University for the time being. We'd lock it up there for now while she, Euan and Mark put together a paper for The British Archaeological Association. Even if the B.A.A. weren't interested, Clare told us, there were other illustrious bodies they could approach.

The curator and I would be credited, of course. Her logic was that the exact location of the find would have to be revealed in their paper, but, until it was published, we could keep it under our hats. After it came out, if any trouble came our way, we'd simply return it to the mine where we found it.

Nobody could argue with that, surely?

Although none of us relished lugging the thing back down underground, we ordered more pints and agreed that we'd reached a fair solution.

All that happened thirty-four years ago. Despite a well-received paper and much publicity on both sides of the Atlantic, any mention of King Arthur's memorial stone still continues to divide opinions in the Archaeological fraternities.

Its 5th century origin isn't in question. The addition evidence provided by the page of *Rex Lamentatio* was pored over by several top History bods and got the stamp of authenticity. What was the problem then? Why aren't these things in pride of place at The British Museum? The answer beggars belief.

You'd have to appreciate the completely bonkers laws in this country relating to 'found' objects of archaeological importance. Rules that were most likely put in place a hundred years ago by a small group of overprivileged, hugely self-important, gentlemen amateurs.

It's thanks to those chaps, that the torn page and the memorial stone were not given the attention they deserved. The manner in which our curator had come by his vellum page and our unauthorised retrieval of Artur's stone, were, in their eyes, the equivalent of inadmissible evidence in a court of law. Our finds, although unarguably important, didn't count because we hadn't gone through the correct channels. This particular 'rule' was probably brought in after someone had finally got fed up with all the illegally obtained Egyptian artifacts turning up in certain world-wide collections and museums.

Artur's stone was returned to its abandoned mine and the pilfered page is in the possession of Mark Hick. The curator felt it was only fair that the bloke who'd actually found the slab should get something out of the whole adventure. Where the two sword holders are is anybody's guess.

Between us though, we'd found the reality behind the ancient legend. King Arthur was a 5th century Cornish warrior. His deeds must have involved not only martial prowess, but also some kind of mystical abilities. He seemed to be respected as a wise ruler too. It's little wonder that he's still remembered today.

A lot has changed in our world since he wielded a sword, but it's still deeds and not words that really make it a better place. Nobody talks about what Arthur said. Like Alfred The Great, or William Tell, it's what he actually did that matters to us.

The Mistletoe Bough

This tale has been doing the rounds here in England for centuries. The Mistletoe Bough is a deeply sad, ghoulish story that's caused many a shudder down the years. The terrible events took place at Beath Hall, South of Penrith in Cumbria.

In the late 18th century, eighteen-year-old Annie Cross was to marry Charles, Lord Beath's only son.

The Beath manor was old and vast. After the wedding feast there, the new bride suggested that they play a game of hide and seek before bedtime. Charles was delighted at the idea of a bit of pre-consummation frivolity, so he readily agreed.

When the guests had shut their eyes and started counting, Annie, in a fever of excitement, ran off to hide. Charles and the guests searched and searched, but she was not located. After many hours, servants joined the hunt as it extended to the grounds. Annie had, seemingly, vanished.

As the hours passed, genuine concern for Annie began to grow. Had she played a trick on them? Could she have simply run away? Days turned to weeks, weeks to months, and (Yes, you've guessed it), months to years. No sign of Annie.

Charles fell into a prolonged state of gloom. He had spent decades looking for his beloved bride. He refused to remarry, never accepting that she'd left him forever. Now, in his late seventies, Charles was called from his study by one of the servants that were clearing the old, unused, attic rooms of his manor.

At the back of a large wardrobe in a dusty garret, two wooden panels had come loose to reveal a small hidden room. When they were removed, a wooden chest was found, the heavy lid decorated with carvings of mistletoe. Until the 19th century, decorative representations of mistletoe were common and not yet associated solely with Christmas.

Inside the chest lay a skeleton in a wedding dress. The deep, blood encrusted scratch marks inside the lid betrayed her vain attempts to lift it.

Charles had his answer at last. Annie's true fate offered him no crumb of comfort though. He died knowing she hadn't left him, but, with no heirs, his line died out. Centuries later, the manor, having changed ownership several times, had fallen into disrepair. Over forty years ago it was bought by a building company, bulldozed, and replaced with a retirement complex.

The tragic irony of her cruel fate and the pathos of her husband's long wait are guaranteed to appeal to the listener. It's a lie though. The truth behind her ghastly death does not paint Charles in a good light.

Twenty years ago, I spent a month in Carlisle searching for any bits of evidence that might still exist concerning poor Annie's fate. It took a lot of legwork, but, eventually, a death certificate, a newspaper report, and some parish records told what really happened to poor Annie.

In 1783, Charles murdered his new bride and a couple of his rich chums helped him cover it up. She had mocked him in front of two of his friends at a gathering months after their wedding. We'll never know what she said that triggered his rage. The four of them had been playing cards. Much drink had been consumed and Charles had not taken kindly to her jokey put down. Without warning, he'd snapped and beaten Annie to death. Charles, it seems, had a bit of a reputation as a hell-raiser and bully-boy. He was no stranger to sudden violent outbursts.

His wealthy land-owning buddies helped him dispose of the corpse in the lake, or somewhere and insisted that Annie had gone missing after their gathering. By all accounts, Charles has played the distraught abandoned husband to perfection.

The skeleton in a wedding dress was a misunderstanding. The poet, Thomas Haynes Bayly, mentions that the skeleton is wearing a bridal wreath, which is a circlet of small white flowers that newlywed girls wore around their foreheads. This, along with the poem's Christmas setting, must have been included to inject some extra poignancy to the story.

At length, an old chest that had long laid hid

Was found in the castle; they raised the lid.

A skeleton form lay mouldering there

In the bridal wreath of that lady fair.

Being a wealthy toff, Charles had no problem covering the whole thing up. They'd taken a set of bones from the local church graveyard, dressed them in one of Annie's gowns, and put them into an old chest. The church was on his land, so no problem there. I mean, he kind of owned the bones anyway. You see, as I discovered later, Charles desperately needed a body to be found.

In reality, the bones were 'discovered' about a year after Annie's brutal death at her husband's hands. Charles had, in fact, casually ordered some servants to clear out a couple of attic rooms so he could store his hunting stuff in them. He knew they would inevitably find the old chest containing the skeleton.

It's clear that Charles had no idea how long a body would take to decompose to bones. If any serious investigation had followed her 'discovery', the authorities would have figured that it takes, at least, fifteen years to become bare bones. Obviously, once the word got out, everyone assumed it had to be the missing woman, especially as the skeleton wore Annie's dress.

Newspaper stories from that era existed on microfilm in Carlisle Library. It was there that I found a report from an old paper, 'The Cumberland Packet', dated Tuesday 17th March 1783. The story, headlined, 'Grave desecrated at a cemetery in Mardale Green.' It seems that there was local outrage because, under cover of night, unknown grave robbers had dug up the skeletal remains of one of the graveyard residents. The ghoulish thieves had, it seems, made a pretty poor job of covering up their misdeed.

The importance of this story would have completely passed me by had it not been for something I'd noticed the previous day at a museum in Kendal.

An 18th century map of the Beath Hall area showed that the tiny village of Mardale Green, along with its churchyard, lay entirely within the Beath Hall estate lands. Hmmm. I thought that was very interesting. A bunch of bones went missing from a graveyard on Charles' land, and, less than a year later, his wife's skeleton turns up in one of his attic rooms.

How did I know when she was 'found'? Whilst in Carlisle, I found copies of the parish death records for, amongst other villages, Mardale Green.

There's an entry for February 1784 that records the burial of Annie (nee Cross), Charles' spouse. The record of their wedding, in January 1783 is also recorded in another section. The unusual aspect of the death record is that although the burial date is listed, the actual date of her death is absent. I've since learned that that was common practice in cases were a body had 'turned up' sometime after the individual had vanished.

Reading the grave robbing report helped me join up the dots. Taking everything I'd learned into account, and especially the phoney decomposed corpse, the finger points very clearly at Charles.

This certainly wasn't the first nor the last time a bunch of over privileged aristos had conspired to hide all traces of a chum's evil deed.

The whole hide-and-seek gone wrong part of the legend was added in to explain away her death as a grisly accident. In those days, way before modern scientific forensics or DNA tests, the word of a posh, titled bloke was quite enough for the authorities.

Annie's death was recorded in the local parish records as accidental, through asphyxiation. It's there for anyone to read. That lie, and her killer's warped sense of entitlement, still annoy the heck out of me.

The dowry dilemma

So? Why did he bother drawing attention to the deceased wife? Why not simply leave the body hidden in the grounds? Well, it was all to do with the law, and specifically Annie's dowry.

At that particular period in English history, a dowry was a decent pot of money given by the bride's dad to his son-in-law. If, however, the loving couple were to separate, or, God forbid, divorce, the husband would have to pay it all back to the girl's father. In his fit of murderous rage Charlie boy hadn't taken this into account. In the cold light of day, after his grim act, Charles could either own up and face a death penalty, or pretend she'd left him and lose the considerable amount of money the dowry brought him.

Quite unwilling to choose either of these paths, the sleazy toff had created a third way. Her 'accidental' death would guarantee that the dowry money remained in his bank account.

So, there it is. A centuries-old haunting legend turns out to be nothing more than a cover up story. The terrible injustice of poor Annie's murder has been gift-wrapped and re-worked as a spooky seasonal yarn. The bad guys were never brought to justice and the victim, a real person, has been reduced to a sort of pathetic ghost train skeleton, a scary punchline.

I have, of course, fleshed out the events of that fateful day when Annie died, but the evidence that would convict her husband is strong. Annie's actual remains were never found. Nobody would try to search for a skeleton that, to all intents and purposes, had already been found.

It beggars belief that, until I did a bit of research, nobody had bothered looking into The Mistletoe Bough story. I'm glad I took the trouble and it's with a great sense of satisfaction that I'm finally able to share it with you.

Traditional Things That Don't Make Sense

They're the kind of questions that challenge established 'truths'. These, seemingly trivial, things get embedded in our cultures in the same way that folklore tales do. In some cases, their veracity is seldom questioned, and, like urban myths and legends, they get adopted as undeniable and...well...normal. For others, there doesn't seem to be either a credible reason or the desire to find one. Here's a few of them.

We need to stop referring to the knuckle bearing side of our hand as its 'back'. They're not the backs of our hands. If anything (When we're standing up) they're the 'outsides'. I can't think of any orientation in which they're the 'backs'.

Your lap is the only section of your body that exists solely when you're sitting down. Otherwise, it's called your legs.

Why does the person who answers the telephone speak first? The onus should be on the caller to speak first, to announce their presence and identify themselves. If the answerer has to say the first thing, "I'm here" would make much more sense than "Hello".

Why aren't coffins buried vertically rather than horizontally? Vertically would save a lot of space.

Why don't battleships fire torpedoes? They seem to work well for submarines.

Why do people use the expression, 'head over heels in love'? Our heads are over our heels most of the time. That's how we're built.

Why do we have earlobes?

Why do we sit down to eat? Standing would be better for our digestive systems.

Why is it considered thoughtless to leave the toilet seat up? Isn't it equally inconsiderate to leave it down?

Why is a ghost considered scary but not a child's imaginary friend?

Why aren't houses fitted with lifts/elevators?

Why do teapots have their spouts on the opposite side to their handles? This makes pouring an awkward lift-and-tip-forward action for your hand. The spout should be on the side of the pot, at a right angle to the handle; a gentle swivel of the wrist would make tea pouring much easier.

Why is standing up supposed to show respect? I'm thinking of standing ovations mainly, but, also, as kids, we were told to stand when a lady came into the room. If there's enough chairs to go around, why bother?

Why do men's and women's clothes button the opposite ways from each other? If they no longer do this, I apologise for being out of touch.

Sod's Law or Supernatural?

Now, in the 21st century, there's piles of stuff that annoy the heck out of everyone. They're the kind of everyday, domestic irritations that make us think we might be in some kind of computer simulation. They're the 'butter side down' toast dropping events that make us question the very fabric of reality. It's almost as if someone or something is manipulating events to piss us off.

A few hundred years ago, these sorts of daily annoyances would probably be explained as witchcraft or other supernatural forces at work. Here's a few of those Victor Meldrew type, 'I don't believe it!' annoyances:

As soon as you ask someone, "What's that noise?", the noise stops.

That annoying, unpleasant kid who always wins raffle prizes.

The act of walking upstairs to do something can temporarily wipe your memory. "Why the heck am I up here?"

When you've achieved something and you want to rub someone's nose in it, they're nowhere to be found.

That magic waft of air that redirects the item you've dropped into the waste bin, causing it to land on the floor next to it instead.

A pedal bin will always remain open if you want the lid to drop to a closed position. The same bin's lid will always drop shut when you need it to remain open.

Oh, no. It's broken! It's either one of two things that needs replacing; there's the expensive thing or the cheap thing, or the thing that's in stock and the one that isn't...Oh, you get the idea.

Whenever you need to look your best, you look like crap.

Spilled liquid always wets your crotch area.

People who don't own dogs are always the ones who get dog crap on their shoes.

Even if you're flexible over the colour, they won't have it in your size (No. Not the dog crap. This is a different example).

Your local supermarket will eventually stop stocking the couple of items you like best.

The people who tell you that they hardly ever have a drink, probably drink more than you do.

Whatever age birthday card you want won't be in stock.

Unless you can manage to grab one for the two seconds that it's edible, a 'ripen in the bowl' peach will either be rock hard or mush.

A lost object will always be found in a location in which you've already looked...

...or it'll be in the last place you look, so always look in the last place first.

The more your friends bang on about how great that TV series is, the more you'll hold out and avoid watching it. Eventually, because you've run out of stuff to binge on, you'll 'give it a go'.

Female TV characters that eat junk food, and ice-cream straight from the tub are always very slim.

Your weekend afternoon nap will immediately trigger your neighbour's lawnmower or electric drill.

Your neighbour's lawnmower or electric drill will immediately trigger your neighbour's yappy dog.

Massively screened TVs are mostly found in very small living rooms.

Your very competitive acquaintances only want to play you at games that they're really good at.

Your very competitive acquaintances will never again offer to play you at the particular game you thrashed them at.

The answer to the clue that you couldn't solve in the cryptic crossword turns out to be an expression used only by people who attended the setter's private school.

That thing you've liked for years, and that you cherished as your own thing, is now, suddenly, insanely popular with billions of folk. And, to make it worse, the media won't stop banging on about how it's 'trending' and that there's, 'a craze' for it. You're so pissed off now that you want to give it up because EVERYBODY is enjoying your thing.

When you just have to complete one simple task, and time is tight, your computer will run an update.

So, that's the list. There are probably thousands more of these. Even the most rational people, at times, think that some kind of force is conspiring against them. Call it Sod's Law, fate, dramatic irony, supernatural forces, or something else. Even in our amazing technical age, it's still difficult to shake off the idea that something's got it in for you.

A Victorian Space Man?

One of the most bizarre imaginary figures in British folklore is undoubtedly Spring-heeled Jack: The Terror of London. From around 1838, early Victorian London saw many reports of a ghostly, white-garbed devil who spat coloured fire, and scared the hell out of folk. There were only ever two actual eyewitness accounts from his 'victims'. Both were female.

According to one of the two women, he wore a skin-tight, one-piece, white outfit. He leapt out of an alley and spat great quantities of blue fire. He then attacked the poor young woman with long metal claws. She was lucky to escape with her life, she claimed. He also wore a large helmet. Otherwise, he seems to have been reconstructed from a diverse set of second and third hand sightings. His costume, headgear and modes of attack varied so much in these accounts that it all has the whiff of an urban legend about it.

Spring-heeled Jack was a popular subject for the theatre of the time. Grisly melodramas, designed to titillate as well as terrify, played to packed houses. Scripts tended to focus on his macabre predilection for the ladies. There were reports of women fainting during shows, and drunken, outraged men leaping onto the stage to confront the fiend. The advances in theatre technology at the end of the 19th Century, certainly helped shape the public's picture of Jack's attacks. Mechanical trap doors, electric lanterns, semi-transparent backlit screens, and many other new devices enabled figures to appear and disappear at will. Horribly realistic make-up and prosthetics made dismemberment and hideous wounds possible.

There were also the beginnings of a move away from the massively exaggerated, melodramatic styles of acting. The theatre craft of Stanislavsky and the works of writers like Ibsen introduced the more 'close up' reality of naturalism. The stage victim's behaviour was much closer to how an audience would imagine themselves reacting. It was all much more scarily real now. Jack's popularity was being fuelled by the very latest theatre craft.

Unlike many other urban legends though, Spring-heeled Jack just would not go away. Accounts of his frightful antics spread from London to other major cities and as far as the Scottish border country. Again, the descriptions offered a wild spectrum of superhuman abilities and crazy outfits. His main aims, it seems, were to scare the living daylights out of ordinary folk, especially women. He continued, in one guise or another, terrorising the population until the beginning of the 20th Century.

Strangely though, as the reports spread out to the counties of England, the claws and fire-breathing disappeared. Over the years (and distance from the capital), he had become more of an acrobatic practical joker. If anything, he'd morphed into a 19th century Free runner, bounding over walls, running at incredible speed, and leaping high buildings. The cheap and popular 'Penny

Horrible' papers of the time helped propagate the increasingly fantastic descriptions of his activities. He'd also become a pretty useful way of controlling the kids: "You mustn't be out after dark, or you might run into Spring-heeled Jack."

I first became aware of this mysterious and disturbing figure when my grandmother told me about him. Margaret was my mother's mum. She'd been a young woman, living in Liverpool when Spring-heeled Jack dropped in there for a brief reign of terror. By that time, late in his career, he wore a one-piece silver suit, strange gold helmet and leaped and bounded over tall buildings. Like everyone else, she'd heard about him from some neighbours who'd been told the tale by someone else. The newspapers' sensational articles also helped boost Jack's credibility in her eyes.

This had been around 1905. Granny told me this story in the mid 1960's. All I could see in my mind's eye was an Apollo astronaut. The one-piece silver suit and helmet played a major part in my belief. The American space missions were something of an obsession for me and my brother back then. What the hell was a 1960's astronaut doing in early 20ᵗʰ Century Liverpool?

Even at that tender age, I was sceptical. I read the newspaper accounts of these Liverpool appearances on microfiche in our nearest library. Sure enough, his apparent apparel was just like granny said. I was stunned! Here was clear evidence of a time-traveller. I had recently read *A Connecticut Yankee in King Arthur's Court*, so my credulity was at an all-time high. Was I the only person who'd twigged that here was proof of backwards time-travel? I wanted to tell everyone. Although Granny's tale was, at least, third hand, for her loving grandson it was gospel. The contradictory descriptions of Jack wearing vampire-like cloaks, bird masks, and skeleton suits, didn't deter me a bit. When Erich von Daniken's book, *Chariots of the Gods* hit the bookstands, any trace of doubt had disappeared. His sensational bestseller showed the world absolute proof that spacemen had visited the ancient civilisations. Why, there were hieroglyphics and tomb carvings to substantiate his claims. An astronaut in old Liverpool would fit right into his thesis.

What were an astronaut's motivations for larking about in Victorian England though? The question had never occurred to me. Had NASA noticed any missing astronauts? I was a restless teenager. I wasn't going to be put off by pertinent questions. The time was right for me to investigate this further. During the next few years though, beer, girls, James Bond films, and Prog. Rock had pushed Spring-heeled Jack down to the bottom of my priorities list. I had only started to think about him again, recently. I think he was simply a product of the late Victorian lust for ghoulishly macabre tales. The more grotesque, the better.

It's likely that, once the newspapers and gossip-merchants got hold of the concept in the 1830's, scores of copy-cats got active. This, along with his usefulness to parents as a child deterrent, and the sheer entertainment value had kept him 'alive' and kicking. He only really fades from sight in the early 20th Century. By that time, the unimaginable terrors of warfare in a post-industrial revolution world had surpassed almost any horrors we could imagine. The radio, gramophones, and early cinema provided new thrills. Entertaining word of mouth stories had lost their impact. Improved photography technology had made it more likely that someone would eventually capture a good image of Spring-heeled Jack. Nobody did. Funny that, isn't it?

We've had a very similar phenomenon more recently. I'm talking about those 'scary' clowns, leaping out of cover, and frightening the bejesus out of kids. Once the idea that clowns can frighten children got out there, hundreds of deeply inadequate men decided to rent Auguste clown costumes, don make-up, and hide in bushes. Like those spooky clowns, Spring heeled Jack seemed to capture the imaginations of people who lacked any imaginations of their own.

Where did the ghoulish clown concept come from? It's been around much longer than people imagine. By the time Stephen King's novel, 'It' was released, in 1986, we'd already had frightening clowns on TV episodes of 'The Avengers' and 'Scooby Doo, Where Are You?' Shows (1968 and 1969, respectively). So, even before the 1960s had ended, the image of a manic menace in make-up was well and truly established.

Anyway, Jack's definitely gone. For a good long while he was a force to be feared. This imaginary terror turned trickster was an urban monster, used as a story to scare children. He was also an invention of minds hungry for stimulation - an instant adrenaline rush in a 19th century world without video games or Ferraris.

Timeline of Investigations

COW TIPPING 1973

THE DISAPPEARING TOILET 1976

THE HAIRY HANDS 1985

THE GHOST OF CASSIOBURY PARK 1985

THE REAL KING ARTHUR 1986

THE BLOODIED FONT 1991

THE LONG BARROW LIGHTS 1991

GHOSTLY NUNS JOIN THE PICNIC 1993

THE WIZARD OF ODD 1998 & 1999

THE PHANTOM LOLLIPOP LADY 1999

THE MISTLETOE BOUGH 2001

SILBURY HILL 2003

PIXIES AND ELVES PICTURE 2010

CINDERELLA'S SLIPPERY LIPS 2018

Recommended Further Reading

Burial Mounds and Decoding the Rituals of Death by Andre Manters

The Quest for Our Neolithic Past by Andre Manters

Wonders of Weather by John Dick

The Meaning of Clouds by John Dick

The Wiltshire Agricultural Gazette

The Wiltshire Downs Farming Fact File 1730 to 2000

Aurora Borealis: A Catalogue of Sightings in England, 1750 to 1888, edited by Steven Berriman

Pixies and Folklore-Folk magazine

Folklore Digest Journal

English Road Marshalls' Handbook (1945 to 1966 editions)

Neolithic News Updates

The Triumphs of Modern Archaeology by Arthur Eeles

Late Roman Britain: The politics of the power shift (Name withheld)

Sacred Woodland Wayfarer by Sarah Cohan

Prehistoric Barrow Legends by Sarah Cohan

Lay Lines of Lincolnshire: A Pub-by-Pub Guide, by Bill Bull

Off the Map by Bill Bull

Life and Death in the Age of Bronze by Owen Trucke

Mysteries of the Untrodden Ways by Roughton Claye

More Mysteries of The Untrodden Ways by Roughton Claye

Journal of Supernatural Routes and Byways

Minutes of the Society for English Civil War Hauntings 1920 to 1927

Inns, Taverns, Ale Houses, and other Haunts by Boyce Surtis

The Forgotten Coaching Inns of Southern England by Boyce Surtis

The Well-Run Library by Edith Brookler

Mediaeval Marriages and other Businesses by Margaret Ryle

Tangled Tapestries: English Nobility Family Trees by Heath G. Leafroche

The Power Behind the Bloodline by Heath G. Leafroche

Town by Town: A Guide to Walking the Western Pig Route by Phil Swinter

Running a Successful Historic Inn by Boyce Surtis

When Spirits Descend by Georgette Kanel

Ozkhadel, Chief Priest by Georgette Kanel

Forging the Forest of Fear by Jules Tjukes

Our Journey to Spiritual Peace magazine (Number 1813, May 1960)

The Wit and Wisdom of the Village Inn by Helen Byhlers

The Solitary Life of the Agricultural Anthropologist by Helen Byhlers

Shadows of the Orange Castle by Karoline Olagen

English County Lives magazine

Mysterious English Countryside magazine

DOROTHY BEAR EDUCATION

Printed in Great Britain
by Amazon

61638923R00098